Trouble in the Halls

Crumberry Chronicles — Book 4

Endorsements

Need a good read-aloud or book series for your middle-schooler? The Crumberry Chronicles is an excellent choice. These books offer young teens an outlet to experience real-life challenges through Jase Freeman, an eleven-year-old with a knack for getting into trouble. Follow him as he faces each challenge and be assured he will be back with more growing pains and lessons learned in each additional book.

When my 5th graders and I began reading the first edition in the Crumberry Chronicles, we could hardly wait to see what was going to happen next. These books are high interest with vivid language and plot twists that keep the reader coming back for more. Jase is a character who is easy to relate to because we all make mistakes and experience inner conflicts in this journey we call life. For so many, it is difficult to talk about our problems and it's wonderful to share such a mix of challenges and chaos and victories together.
—**Debbie Snowden**, teacher and parent

Shelley Pierce has written four amazing, middle-school appropriate, fiction books. The Crumberry Chronicles series is not only entertaining, but also aids in spiritual growth for the reader. These books offer middle-school-age children an escape to Jase's world. Here they realize

that all of their fears and problems are shared with their now friend, Jase. It gives children the opportunity to get advice from Jase when they feel like they can't get it anywhere else. Most importantly, it gives children the chance to learn about God in a non-threatening way. Through these books, the reader learns God never leaves us. We get a better understanding, no matter the situation we are in, that we can always stop and pray. He hears us. These books are a must read, and I keep them available to my own children as well as my students.
—Lori Swatzell, Assistant Administrator, High School Advisor

Shelley makes the characters in her books come alive while keeping the memory of Jase's dad actively a part of the story. Emotions range from emphatic sorrow to enthusiastic joy. As a middle-school teacher, I hear my students discussing many of the topics in Shelley's books—Trail Life, sports, science fair projects, substitute teachers, outdoor adventures, and bullying. I love that the Lord is glorified throughout The Crumberry Chronicles.
—Virginia Cooter

The Crumberry Chronicles series tells the amazing story of the struggles and triumphs of Jase Freeman. The stories in these books give children a place of encouragement as they relate to all Jase experiences. Every parent needs to read and enjoy these books before giving them to their child to read. The stories will provide great discussion starters!
I know they are written for middle-school kids, but this seventy-nine-year-old sure enjoys them.
—Peggie Mothershed

Let's face it. Middle school is hard. Juggling schedules, time, friends, activities, and home life can be a struggle. The Crumberry Chronicles will capture your attention

from the first chapter. You will be able to relate to the situations Jase finds himself in. The chapters are short and always leave you wanting to read "just one more." You don't have to be in middle school to get caught up in this series. Shelley Pierce's writing captures you immediately. Read one book and you'll be hungry for more.
—Teresa Henry

I feel as though I know Jase Freeman. Shelley Pierce has introduced me to a character I like very much. As he matures emotionally and morally, and as he faces challenges, he has opened my mind and heart more fully to understand issues youth encounter. His loyalty to friends and his tenderness toward those being bullied is touching. I anxiously await more days learning from Jase.
—Sharon King, retired after forty years at my dream profession. Teacher.

I absolutely love Shelley Pierce's books and her unique style of writing! The Crumberry Chronicles series is so relatable, especially to middle schoolers, but even as a high schooler. I still enjoy reading them. It is sometimes hard to find good, clean books, but when I pick up these books up, I can't seem to put them down!
—Brilyn R., 14

Shelley Pierce takes readers on an emotional journey through some of life's obstacles through the eyes of middle schooler Jase Freeman. People of all ages can relate to Jase and learn how to follow Christ in every situation. Jase shows how God can use everyone, no matter the age, to do the right thing. Every person should RUN and grab the entire Crumberry Chronicles series. Read the books as a family or on your own, but everyone needs to read them!
—Joy Turner, Assistant PreK Director/PreK Teacher and Mom

Trouble in the Halls

Crumberry Chronicles—Book 4

Shelley Pierce

Copyright Notice

Trouble in the Halls Crumberry Chronicles—Book 4

Cover and Interior Design: Cheryl Childers

Editor(s): Cristel Phelps, Deb Haggerty

Author Represented By: Hartline Literary Agency

PUBLISHED BY: Elk Lake Publishing, Inc., 35 Dogwood Drive, Plymouth, MA 02360, 2021

Library Cataloging Data

Names: Pierce, Shelley (Shelley Pierce)

Trouble in the Halls Crumberry Chronicles—Book 4 / Shelley Pierce

274 p. 23cm × 15cm (9in × 6 in.)

ISBN-13: 978-1-64949-417-7 (paperback) | 978-1-64949-418-4 (trade paperback) | 978-1-64949-419-1 (e-book)

Key Words: Middle-grade; bullying; inferiority complex; friendship; relationships; stepparents; family

DEDICATION

To the noble men and women of the American military who stepped up to fight against evil in the Afghanistan war, to their families who kept the home fires burning, and to the One True God who continues to work all things for good to those who love him.

Our gratitude is not enough.

ACKNOWLEDGMENTS

Thank you, Deb Haggerty and Elk Lake Publishing, for investing in me and Jase Freeman's story. I truly love you and am blessed to be a part of the Elk Lake family.

Cristel Phelps, you never cease to amaze me with your God-given talents and eye for what makes a great story. You certainly make me look like I know what I'm doing. Thank you for loving Jase and finding value in The Crumberry Chronicles.

Thank you, Cheryl L. Childers, for your wonderful creativity in cover design. You masterfully depict the story inside, and I don't know how you manage, but your art flows beautifully from one Crumberry cover to the next.

Special thanks to Brilyn R. for offering her well-thought-out suggestions and impressions. You are *Trouble in the Hall*'s first reader, and the story is far better because of you.

Tommy Pierce, how can I begin to express my love and gratitude for the many ways you fuel story. The long car rides for brainstorming and statements such as "That doesn't sound like something Jase would say," enabled *Trouble in the Halls* to unfold. You are my Forever.

Thank you, Lord, for keeping your promise to work in all things to bring good to those who love you.

CHAPTER ONE

Every sixth grader, at one point or another, believes middle school exists to torture innocent kids.

Why else would such things as algebra, rope climbing in gym class, and the options in the cafeteria be realities? Peer pressure and the painful need to either fit in or blend in.

Like.

Every.

Day.

Jase Freeman, resident struggler to blend in, found himself the object of attention once again. Each class more uncomfortable than the one before, he exhaled as he stepped in line to take his chances in the cafeteria. He pulled at the collar of his T-shirt and used his sleeve to swipe across his forehead.

"Well, it's about time! Where have ya been? Hiding out or taking bows?" Jase's best friend, Steve, waved his arm wildly as he called out to Jase to take his place at the table.

"What are you even talking about? Take a bow? Hardly." Jase noticed the eyes of his friends. Eyes just like everyone else today.

Steve, Danny, and Deirdre examined him as if he were some new breed of insect no one had ever seen before. And Haley? Well, Haley looked down at her tray. Maybe she was examining the presence of UFO's ... Unidentified Food Organisms.

Trouble in the Halls

Deirdre elbowed her twin brother, Danny, as he snickered.

Jase stood by the table, holding his tray with sweaty hands. He had not yet decided whether he would sit here or search for a corner table for solitude. A quick scan of the lunchroom proved the impossibility of a gawk-free seat.

He slid in between Steve and Danny and shoved a tater tot into his mouth.

"Anybody do anything fun over the break?" he inquired in between munching.

"My grandmother gave me illustrated classics for Christmas. I read the entire set! I can't choose a favorite. I think I'll read them again before I decide." Everyone knew of Deirdre's love of books.

Steve rolled his eyes. Everyone knew of his disdain for books.

"Well? Are you going to tell us?" Deirdre batted her eyes.

"Yeah. You should tell us." Jase wondered if Danny ever had a thought of his own.

"Y'all need to grow up. She's just a friend and ... and we're not in third grade."

Deafening silence fell across the table. Friends stopped chewing. And breathing.

"What?"

"What do you mean 'what?' What are you talking about? Who is just a friend? Uh-oh. Jasey must have a crush!" Steve taunted.

Haley blushed.

"Shut up, Steve. And grow up!"

Steve shrugged.

Haley cleared her throat, "Uh—hem, you might as well tell them your news."

"Oh ... you mean my Grandpa Rocky? Yeah! My mom's dad knocked on our door. Everyone thought he died in a bad wreck lots of years ago. But nope. Talk about weird. Mom cried ... well, everyone cried. Not me, though. I didn't cry."

"You're rambling." Deirdre smirked.

"Yeah. Rambling." Danny agreed.

"Uh-huh. You are." Steve shrugged.

Jase wondered if Haley would help. Instead of speaking up, she giggled and popped a grape into her mouth.

"Okay, already. My mom and Mr. Tims are going to get married. Soon."

"Yeah, we know. Can't decide if you're a lucky dog or whether you'll *need* some luck." Steve elbowed Jase.

"What does luck have to do with it?"

Steve grinned. "You really don't get it, do you, little buddy? Your news splits Crumberry Middle School wide open. Some think you're gonna get special treatment, and they're already mad. Others think you're gonna get special treatment, and they're already jealous. All I know is I'm glad I'm not you."

Why do adults have to complicate life for helpless sixth grade boys who are trying to blend in?

CHAPTER TWO

"Did you hear what he said?"

"Yeah. What a weirdo."

"Who says 'you guys' and his accent ... seriously? Who says, 'you guys'?"

"Weirdos."

The boy walked alone. Did he hear what the girls said?

He walked past the girls, then past a group of guys. Watching his feet and the floor ahead of them. Slow, careful steps.

The boys watched him walk by. They didn't speak until he turned the corner down the hall.

"Who is he?"

"I dunno. Some new kid. I heard he came from Canada."

"Anybody know his name?"

"Haven't heard."

"Probably some Canadian name."

Jase heard the girls. Saw the new kid. The boys talked about the new kid as well. He wondered if the boy no one knew really came from Canada. And he wondered why saying 'you guys' was a problem.

The way he figured, there was room at Crumberry Middle School for a new kid.

He would worry about Canada, and 'you guys,' and the new guy later. This day had enough 'weird' going around without asking for a second helping.

CHAPTER THREE

"Well, look. There he is. The Favored One."

"Yeah, I heard his 'A' is already written in the algebra gradebook."

"Hey, maybe he can get a hold of the semester test."

Jase curled his lip at his classmates as he walked to his desk.

"Grow up," he jeered.

"Big talk for a small guy."

"Mr. Tims put a ring on it ... he's empowered."

A surge of anger bubbled inside Jase. "I think you should shut up."

The sound of his own voice rang in his head. He knew he sounded weak. He deserved the laughter that followed. He expected someone to say "No, you shut up." No one spoke. Instead, they laughed. A lot.

"How about you share the joke?" Mr. Tims shuffled in, hung his cane on a coat hook by the door, and stood by his desk. Most kids in Crumberry Middle School knew his story. How he served in Afghanistan with the Marine Corps, suffered a wound, and overcame the injury by walking again when doctors said he never would. Mr. Tims gave God credit for being able to put one foot in front of the other.

Argh! Can this day get any worse?

The laughter faded, and the students sat up straight.

"Well, okay. How about we get started. Did anything go wrong over the break?" Mr. Tims was known for his famous 'what went wrong' question. He taught his classes to learn from unfortunate circumstances.

Yeah. You put a ring on it.

Mandy nearly jumped out of her seat as she raised her hand, stretching as if she wanted to touch the ceiling.

"This ought to be good."

"There's no telling ..."

"Okay, boys. Let her speak," Mr. Tims chuckled. "Mandy, we can't wait to hear what you have to say."

"Well," Mandy took a deep breath. "My dog opened one of my gifts before Christmas morning. She pulled it out from under the tree, all the way to my room! Under my bed! She ripped the paper off all by herself. Mom saw the paper and blamed me. I tried to tell her Dolly did it, but she didn't believe me. Then Mom asked me why I blamed the dog."

"Ouch. Did you get in trouble?"

"Almost. Dolly saved the day. She heard Mom fussing and she ran under the bed and came out with a pair of red, fuzzy slippers in her mouth. Mom laughed, and I laughed, and Dolly dropped the slippers at Mom's feet."

"Did you learn anything from Dolly's adventure?"

"I didn't. But Mom did. She learned Dolly is a sneak, and I tell the truth."

"Well, there you have it. Always tell the truth, so when your dog steals a Christmas gift, or eats your homework, you won't get the blame. Open your textbook to chapter forty-three. Let's see how far we can get before the bell rings."

Someone whispered, "He said *ring*."

Giggles and snorts rolled across the room.

"Jokes again? Anyone want to let me in on it?" Mr. Tims frowned.

His frown replaced the laughter with the sound of textbook pages flipping open to chapter forty-three.

CHAPTER FOUR

You could at least go the speed limit. Buses are allowed to go faster than five miles-per-hour.

He closed his eyes and pretended to go to sleep. The seat jostled when someone plopped down next to him.

"Did you meet the new kid? Austin. Wait, no. Justin. Oh, um. I think it's Harry ... no, no, wait. Harrison. That's it. Harrison! Did you meet Harrison?"

Jase opened one eye and squinted at Haley.

"Did you hear me?" she cupped her hands around her mouth and spoke louder. "I said, did you ..."

"I heard you. Did I meet Austin Justin Harry Harrison? No, I didn't. I saw him, though. And I heard kids laughing at him."

"Why do boys have to be so mean?" Haley folded her arms and squinted back.

"Who said it was boys? Well ... it *was* boys, but not just boys. Girls too."

"Poor, Harry. Uh, Harrison. Do you suppose anyone befriended him? I mean, he's moved here all the way from Colorado."

"Canada. They said Canada."

"Canada. Colorado. What's it matter?"

"I'm sure it matters to him. I don't know if he's got any friends. I didn't see him the rest of the day." Jase rested his head on the back of the seat and closed his eyes once again.

"Well, we should ask him to eat lunch with us tomorrow. Don't you think?" Seeing his eyes were closed, she grunted and raised her voice. "Jase! I said ..."

"I heard you. Yes. Harry. Lunch. Tomorrow."

"Harrison."

"Harrison."

"Lunch."

"Yeah, yeah. Tomorrow."

Haley shrugged. And she sighed as she shook her head. She wondered why she put up with him. He could be persnickety and sometimes rude. He had a fun side that made the rude side tolerable. She wished she could understand his cranky moments.

She and Jase Freeman, friends since second grade, knew each other well. She knew he was often moody on the bus ride to Juniper Street. She knew he spent too much time thinking and rethinking and then thinking some more. And she knew, sooner or later, he would tell her the thoughts he was currently rethinking.

CHAPTER FIVE

"What do you think, Jase? Gray or mauve?"

"I think you need to ask Aunt Christy. What would I know about it?"

"My dress is ivory with light pink lace ..."

"Mauve? What's mauve?"

"Actually, it's light mauve. Very light." She continued speaking as if speaking to herself. She walked to the closet and retrieved her wedding dress. She hung it on the door frame and held two pieces of cloth next to it. One gray, one light mauve. "Hmm, I think gray. What do you think?"

"Seriously. Not my thing, Mom. Facetime Aunt Christy and see what she thinks."

She tussled her son's hair as she reached for her cellphone. "You're so techy. I wouldn't have thought of Facetime."

Jase went to the kitchen for a snack. He could hear his mom chattering away and Aunt Christy saying stuff like "Oh, it's beautiful!" and "I like the gray."

He paused long enough to look back at his mom. He remembered when sadness stole her laughter and longing snatched her joy. He whispered a thank you prayer, knowing God saw the cloud that once hovered over their home. He knew God heard his prayer for help. Yes, it was good to see the sparkle of happiness in her eyes again.

Chesty followed at his heals. "How was your day? I could have done without most of mine."

Trouble in the Halls

The chubby English bulldog puppy sat and wagged his tail at his owner. Jase patted him on the head and grabbed an apple from the basket on the table.

"Come on, boy, you can help me with my homework."

They trekked down the hall to the bedroom.

"Rawwwk!" Lecty, an eclectic parrot, greeted them as they entered.

"You two are the best friends a guy could ever have. Always happy to see me, never laughing at me. And you don't ask what color goes better with an ivory wedding dress."

"Rawwwk! Ohhhh! I like grey!"

"Silly old bird."

Chesty chased his tail, circling until he slowed enough to lay down in a little ball.

"The wedding is this weekend. Sometimes I'm glad. Sometimes not so much."

Chesty yawned.

Jase sat at his desk and held his picture of his dad in dress blues. His dad thought of everything while deployed in Afghanistan. He wrote many letters, telling Jase most of the things a boy needs to hear from his dad. He even wrote, that if he didn't make it home from war, he wanted Jase and his mom to live a happy life and not let sadness take over.

He knew his dad would approve of Mr. Tims ... Sully. After all, Sully and his dad were best friends. Marines, deployed to Afghanistan. Battle buddies.

Why am I not sure about this ... this wedding?

"Put your phone away while we're eating."

"Can I send one more text? Steve will wonder what happened to me."

"One more. Then put it away. You know it doesn't belong at the table."

Jase pressed send and put his phone in his pocket.

"How was school? Glad you're back?"

"Real funny, Mom. School is more stressful than it was before ..."

He took a bite and stared at his plate.

"Before what?"

Maybe if I ignore her she will move to another subject.

"Jase. Before what?"

He rearranged the food on his plate. "It's not important. Just getting back into school after sleeping in and being at Pop and Juju's farm. I wasn't ready."

"Anything else bothering you?"

"Well. Yes. Everyone knows."

"Knows what?"

"Mom, really? Ivory dress?"

"Oh. Well, I still don't see a problem."

"Kids at school stared at me like I'm some kind of freak. My mom is marrying the algebra teacher."

"I'm sorry, Son. They will move on to something or someone else before long."

"I guess. Until then they will look at me like I've grown an extra eye in the middle of my forehead."

"Don't be so dramatic. Finish your supper."

He went to bed wondering how long before the kids at school would move on. He wondered why his mom thought he was being dramatic.

And he wondered if Austin Justin Harry Harrison would be the one to take the attention.

CHAPTER SIX

She followed the sound of laughter and found Harrison Peterson cramming books into his locker. With each book he added, another fell to the floor.

He grunted and tried again.

"Might help if you were organized." Haley tried to hide her amusement.

He stopped stuffing and glared at her.

"Wow. Okay."

He managed to get the last book in and slam the door without smashing any fingers.

"What's your plan?"

"I'm going to class." He finally spoke.

"I figured. I meant what's your plan when you need another book?"

He grunted again.

"My name is Haley."

"I'm Harrison."

"If you want, you can eat with my friends and me at lunch. You know, sit at our table."

"Thanks. Maybe."

And he walked away.

She shrugged her shoulders and headed off to class.

Trouble in the Halls

Mrs. Zimmers clicked her tongue on the roof of her mouth and wrapped her ruler on her desk.

"Students! Simmer down. Did you leave your self-control at home today?"

Fidgeting and whispering came to a standstill. All eyes forward.

Jase welcomed normalcy. Even if it meant science class.

Most kids at Crumberry Middle School were afraid of Mrs. Zimmers. With her perfect posture, stern tone of voice, and the lingering scent of hand sanitizer, she controlled the room.

Jase got all the normality he needed for the next hour and a half. He actually relaxed, knowing he wasn't getting the stink eye from anyone, and no one would dare make a wise crack under penalty of whatever Mrs. Zimmers deemed proper.

First period ended, and Mrs. Zimmers stood at the door at the end of class, nodding at each student passing by. She stopped nodding when Jase approached.

"Please stay a moment, Mr. Freeman."

He took a few steps back and waited. *Whatever it is, I didn't do it. Not this time. Not the first week back after break.*

The lines on her face softened as she smiled.

"Hardship builds character. I'm aware of the engagement and your classmates' remarks. This is just one more character-building obstacle of life, Jase. Be encouraged. Everything will be okay."

"I might have enough character for three of four people by the time I graduate the sixth grade."

"Keep your sense of humor. Laughter is a gift. Hold your head high. You're an overcomer."

"Thank you." Jase stepped toward the hall. "Mrs. Zimmers?"

"Yes?"

"How long before they quit staring?"

"I do not know," She shook her head. "Hold your head high and keep your sense of humor."

He wrinkled his face and raised his eyebrows one at a time, back and forth.

She laughed at the expression, and he went on his way.

To face the day.

And the faces of Crumberry Middle School.

CHAPTER SEVEN

Jase saw him as soon as he stepped into literature class.

Austin Justin Harry Harrison.

Poor kid.

Whispers and stares were present, but Jase Freeman wasn't on the receiving end. A wave of guilt washed over his sigh of relief.

So, he did it.

Without thinking.

Walked right up to the new kid.

"Hey. I'm Jase."

A hush fell across the room.

"I'm Harrison."

"You weren't in this class yesterday."

"Ya. I know. I went to the wrong room."

Muffled snorts and snickers sprinkled across the room.

"Don't worry. It won't last."

"What won't last?"

Jase nodded at their classmates. "The attention. Try to ignore them."

"Could be worse, I guess. Better than a poke in the eye with a sharp stick, ya know."

"Huh?"

"Never mind."

"They'll move on to someone else soon. Maybe even back to me."

Harrison lifted his gaze from his desktop to look at Jase.

"You?"

"Yeah. It happens. Hey, want to eat lunch with my friends and me? They can be pretty weird, but it's better than eating alone."

"Some girl named Haley invited me to eat with her today."

"Yeah, Haley. She's one of the gang."

"Oh. Okay. Thanks."

Jase sat down and pulled his literature book out of his backpack.

He wondered where this kid came from. He wondered why someone would poke him in the eye with a sharp stick.

And he wondered why Haley was anxious to have Austin Justin Harry Harrison sit with them at lunch.

CHAPTER EIGHT

"So, I heard you moved here from Canada or Colorado. Which is it?" Jase and Harrison took their place in the line leading into the cafeteria.

"Neither."

Awkward pause.

Man of little words. Or rude. Or both.

"So. Where are you from?"

"Minnesota."

"*Hey, you guys*! Look who's in line."

"The freak!"

Harrison looked forward, as if he didn't hear the talk.

"Go back to Canada, weirdo."

Jase turned around to face them.

"What's your problem? Leave him alone."

"Why don't you make us?" Andrew, an eighth grader, stepped forward.

"I'm not afraid of you. Leave him alone."

Andrew pointed his finger at Jase, holding it a little too close to Jase's nose.

"Maybe you should keep your nose in your own business." And with those words, Andrew flicked the tip of Jase's nose.

And then it happened.

Action.

Actually ... reaction.

He shoved Andrew as hard as he could. Andrew tumbled backwards, knocking the obnoxious taunting bunch of kids down like bowling pins. A sneaker sailed through the air and cell phones were forced out of pockets. Jase wasn't sure who was more surprised. Andrew, the guilty bunch of bowling pins, or himself.

"Jase Freeman! What are you doing?" The familiar voice of Mr. Tims echoed down the hall, all the way to Jase's ears. He looked up to see his teacher-soon-to-be-stepdad hobble as fast as his cane would allow. Red faced. Toward Jase.

He's moving right along.

"Mr. Tims, I ..."

"Don't speak." Mr. Tims face grew deeper red.

"But I ..."

"Do not speak. Come with me."

Jase followed him into the first unoccupied classroom.

Mr. Tims heaved a loud sigh.

"Sully, I ..."

"It's Mr. Tims while we are at school. I saw you, Jase. I watched you shove that boy. What were you thinking?"

"I was thinking I didn't like him touching ..."

"Stop. It doesn't matter. You know better."

"But it *does* matter!"

"Don't talk back. Like it or not, we are both going to be on trial after this weekend. Every kid at CMS expects me to give you special treatment. I hope you know I will not show favoritism."

"I didn't ask for special treatment. Don't you even care about my side of what happened?"

"Will it make a difference? Does it make what you did okay?"

"Mr. Tims. They were making fun of Harrison, the new kid. I told them to stop."

"Okay. So, you shoved them?"

"No. That's not what happened. Andrew put his finger in my face. He touched my ..."

"I don't want to hear any more. Go to Principal Drew's office. Let him handle you."

Jase held his breath and stepped back into the hall.

"Oh, and Jase," Mr. Tims clenched his jaws. "You may as well know now, as my stepson I will expect you to walk the line. I can't be embarrassed by your behavior."

Jase began the long walk to Principal Drew's office. With each step he took, he wondered why Sully refused to listen to him. He wondered why he had never seen this side of Mr. Tims before.

And he wondered if he should tell his mom about this or if Sully was dialing her cell phone this very minute.

CHAPTER NINE

"Take a seat." Principal Drew tap, tap, tapped on his keyboard. Jase had never actually seen Principal Drew *working*. He honestly thought the principal's job was to sit in his office waiting on wayward students, walk the halls giving firm facial expressions to kids having too much fun, and to make boring morning announcements over the PA.

He had been here before. In this chair. Waiting for the long arm of the law to reach out and grab him. Even so, he had never noticed the superhero action figures lining the top shelf of the bookcase or the odd-looking picture of a face with lips where ears should be and an eyeball in place of lips.

He sat like a statue and didn't move a muscle as he breathed. He wasn't afraid. After all, he had done nothing wrong. What self-respecting guy would allow some big mouth to flick the tip of his nose? Seriously, though.

And so, he waited.

Tap, tap, tap.

Breathe in. Breathe out.

Tap, tap, tap.

"Ahem, excuse me sir." Andrew stood at the office door.

"Take a seat." Tap, tap, tap.

Oh, I can just hear it. He started it, Principal Drew. I was minding my own business, and he just shoved me. He thinks he's special because Mr. Tims is gonna be his stepdad. I'm innocent.

Jase looked out the window behind Principal Drew's desk. He watched the January snow falling without a care in the world. He wondered if he would ever know the feeling.

"I understand you boys have a problem?" He looked left to right. Then right to left.

Silence.

"I'm not even going to ask for the details because it doesn't matter."

But it does matter.

"Andrew, you've been in and out of my office since sixth grade. Seems you're always picking on someone smaller or newer or whatever you think is different. I've made many attempts to help you change the error of your ways."

Andrew didn't look up.

"And Jase. I've seen you here as well."

Jase tried to count the snowflakes.

"I don't have time to listen to explanations. Here's the deal. I'm not sending you home or to in-school suspension. Instead, beginning tomorrow through the end of the week, you two will eat lunch together. At the table in the front of the cafeteria. Maybe by the end of the week, you'll be friends. Be warned, if there is a single disturbance between you, you will spend the remainder of the semester together in suspension. Do I need to remind you the semester just began?"

"No, sir." Came the reply in unison.

Not the Table of Shame. With Andrew.

"Go eat while you still have time."

The boys stood, and without a word, stepped into the hall to begin the walk back to the cafeteria.

It's only three days. Just three days of shame ... I mean lunch with Mr. Tough Guy. I can do this.

"It's my fault. I'm sorry." Harrison was seated in between Haley and Danny.

"You didn't ask for help. My choice." Jase sat across from them.

"What happened? What did Drew say? Is Mr. Tims still mad?" Jase couldn't tell if Steve cared or just wanted to hear the details of his punishment.

"Are you headed to suspension? Will we ever see you again?"

"Don't sound so excited, Steve. No. I'm not going to suspension. I get to eat lunch with Andrew the rest of the week."

A gasp moved in a wave around the table. All eyes on Jase.

Deirdre spoke first. "Not the Table of Shame!"

"What's the Table of Shame?" Harrison had a lot to learn.

"Dude, seriously. Say it ain't so." Steve went all googly-eyed.

"You guys. What is the Table of Shame?"

Deirdre sighed and pointed.

There it stood.

Alone.

In the front of the cafeteria. Empty seats on either side, the table patiently awaited the arrival of this semester's rebels.

"Well, at least it's not as bad as a poke in the eye with a sharp stick." Harrison shrugged and ate his lunch.

The table of friends looked at this new kid with mixed expressions of confusion and amusement.

Jase wondered if he should have kept his nose in his own business and let Austin Justin Harry Harrison find out for himself there are worse things than a sharp stick in the eye.

And why is he sitting next to Haley?

CHAPTER TEN

Jase would have paid a thousand bucks to be able to skip algebra. Well ... he would if he'd had a thousand bucks.

Since escaping could not be an option, he put his best foot forward. Held his head high, as Mrs. Zimmers advised. And tried to find something, *anything*, humorous about the events of the day.

Determined to stay quiet and to himself, Jase sat down and opened his algebra book. Pencil sharpened and ready.

It's go time.

"How about some decimal fun? Are you up for it?" Mr. Tims held a stack of worksheets in the air.

"What does how loud a sound is have to do with algebra?" Jase didn't even raise his hand. *Let's see if humor helps a bad day.*

"Uh, good one, Jase. But let's try to focus. For those of you not following, a decibel measures sound—a decimal, for our purposes today, helps us measure numbers by ten."

"Will your decibels go up if we get our decimals wrong?"

Nervous laughter rippled across the room.

Mr. Tims looked at Jase without speaking. Students fidgeted in their seats.

Seconds passed.

Ten.

Twenty.

A nauseating, eternity-inducing thirty seconds ticked by without a word spoken. Possibly without a single person in the room exhaling.

Jase bit the inside of his lip and wondered why he followed Mrs. Zimmers advice.

"If you pay attention, I believe each of you will have no trouble learning the proper use and placement of the tiny dot we refer to as a decimal point." Mr. Tims removed his gaze from Jase. "Concentrate in class and you will not have homework today. Goof off," his gaze returned, "and I will be sure you have enough homework you'll not have any time for gaming."

Message sent and received, loud and clear.

Mr. Tims handed a stack of papers to each kid in the front row and gave instructions to take one and pass the rest back.

If the air had a color, it would have been puke green. Or maybe slimy gray. Either way, it would be an unhappy shade of sour.

Laughter had been a hallmark of Mr. Tims's class. A way of relieving the pressure of equations and numbers and letters. Lightheartedness had now been replaced by confusion. Jase knew he couldn't be the only kid who noticed the new, stressed-out Mr. Tims.

Or maybe no one else cared.

But Jase was certain, in a class of twenty-eight kids, at least 0.75 of the kids were as confused as he.

Trying to be funny wasn't his only mistake. He made another mistake. A mistake he was totally ignorant of making. Unbeknownst to him, there were no longer twenty-eight kids in his algebra class. Now there were twenty-nine.

For there, in the back row, right hand corner, sat Harrison Peterson.

CHAPTER ELEVEN

The days crawl but the weeks fly. His dad had described deployed life in one of the letters from Afghanistan. For a middle-school kid, the hours crawl but the day ... well, the day crawls too.

Gym class. Possibly the best part of his school day. No, definitely. Definitely the best part of today.

"Get busy! Warm up drills! Everybody on the line!" Coach K barked the orders.

Jase ran the drills with the rest of his gym class until Coach called for shooting drills to begin.

Balls bouncing. Never in unison. Flying through the air in a race for the goal. Two balls collide and sail off in opposite directions.

Jase waited for the perfect moment to take a shot. The swoosh of the ball sliding through the net gave him the confidence he needed to take another shot. He knew his skills were hidden in the world of video games. Whether in solitude or playing virtually against others, no crowd would ever chant his name or cheer over a game well played.

He didn't care, though. If no crowd could cheer, there would be no jeering either.

Dribble, dribble, shoot. Dribble, dribble, shoot. Dribble, dribble ... wait. What?

Jase looked over to see Mr. Tims and Coach K, standing at the locker room door.

Talking.

With eyes darting Jase's way in an I'm-looking-I'm-not-looking kind of way.

Dribble, dribble, shoot ...

Oh, great. Over there talking about me.

Dribble, dribble, dribble, dribble.

He doesn't even know the whole story. He didn't bother to find out.

Shoot.

And why does Coach K need to know my business?

Dribble, dribble, shoot.

Maybe Coach will listen to my side.

Dribble, dribble, shoot.

Yeah. That's it. And he will tell Sully, and I won't be in trouble anymore.

Dribble, dribble.

"How's it going?" Coach K towered over Mr. Tims.

"Getting back into the swing of things is no picnic. I think their brains are still on break." Mr. Tims nodded toward the weaving, dribbling packs of kids.

"They'll readjust. Give them time. Speaking of time. This weekend?"

"You'll be there, right?"

"Wouldn't miss it."

Dribble, dribble, shoot.

Teachers stick together, though.

Shoot.

They've probably decided my fate.

Dribble, dribble, dribble.

I guess the whole school knows my business.

Shoot.

"Couldn't be happier for you."

"Thanks. I better get back to grading papers."

"And I think these kids are warmed up enough for a quick game."

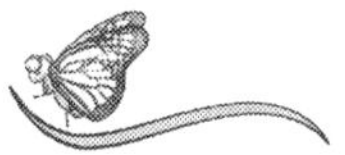

There he goes. My stepdad, who tells my business to anyone who will listen.

CHAPTER TWELVE

She walked with Harrison to his locker, jibber jabbering about the day. He listened, or at least she thought he was listening.

"And I heard Jase caused a scene in algebra. You were in there, weren't you? Did he cause a scene?"

"Eh. Not much. A few low remarks, and Mr. Tims gave him the stare down. He left class as soon as the bell rang. I don't think you need to worry about Jase. He can take care of himself. I mean, when that kid, what's his name ... Andrew? When Andrew started mouthing off, I told Jase not to worry about it. I told him I can take care of it myself, but he didn't listen. I think he likes the attention he got by jumping in where he didn't belong."

"Mmm, that doesn't sound like Jase."

"You're calling me a liar? I was there. You weren't. So, believe me or don't. I don't care."

"Wow, Harrison. Why the chip on your shoulder?"

"No chip. Just saying. Jase likes attention and will make his own drama. I am good at reading people."

Haley pondered what he said. Her brain sent exclamation marks of protest to her heart. But ... he sounded genuine.

Did Jase step in where he wasn't needed or wanted? Does Jase need the attention?

The bus pulled out to start the trek of depositing kids home after the long school day. Jase slid onto the seat behind Haley.

"Hey, you okay?" She smiled at him.

"I'm fine."

"Are you worried?"

"About what?"

"Your mom. Trouble. Mr. Tims. You know ..."

"Mom doesn't get off work until six tonight. I have time to think of a defense. I'm not sure she even knows."

"Why did you step in? I mean, couldn't Harrison have handled it?"

"I dunno. I didn't think about it. Just felt right."

"What did he do? I mean, Harrison."

Jase scowled. "Why do you even care, Haley? What does it matter?"

"Wow, okay. Never mind. Forget it."

"Fine with me."

Jase wondered why she had so many questions. What is it about this Austin Justin Harry Harrison guy that made her curious? Had they not been friends long enough she didn't need to ask all these questions?

Back at Crumberry Middle School, after the final bus pulled away, Harrison Peterson stepped into the classroom and cleared his throat.

"Excuse me, Mr. Tims? Do you have a minute?"

"Sure, Harrison. Come on in. What's on your mind?"

"Well, what happened today in the lunch line. Andrew didn't deserve what happened. I'm not sure why Jase shoved him. Andrew asked if I wanted to sit with him at lunch, and Jase went off on him. I thought you needed to know."

CHAPTER THIRTEEN

He finished his homework. Washed a load of towels. Set the table, made rice, and heated a can of beef stew.

The lock on the front door clicked, and Jase greeted his mom by taking her coat.

"Supper's ready. Beef stew and rice."

"Thank you! Sounds good."

She must not know. She's too happy to know.

"How was work?"

"Can't complain. How about school?"

"No good stories to tell?" asked Jase.

"No. Just another day. How about school."

He spooned a large bite and pointed at his mouth as he chewed, shrugging a can't-talk-with-my-mouth-full shrug.

He believed his delay in answering his mom's probing question about school had worked. From delay to overlooked, threat averted.

Her cellphone chimed with Sully's personal tone, volume rising with each second the call went unanswered.

"Aren't you going to answer your cell?" He focused on keeping his voice calm and steady.

"No phones at the table. I'll call him back."

Threat. Averted.

"Where were we? Oh, yeah. School. How was your day? Do you have much homework?"

"I finished it as soon as I got home."

"Good, you can help me with a few wedding details."

"Seriously, Mom. Light mauve or gray. You need to choose."

"Aunt Christy settled the dress dilemma yesterday. We need to go over your part of the vows."

"Wait, what? *My* part? No, no, no, no, no. I don't have a part. This is between you and Sully."

"If we are going to be family, I think you need to have a part as well."

"Mom! This isn't the kind of thing you spring on a guy. I mean ... whoa. No. Just no."

"I didn't think you would protest so loudly. Maybe just think about it, okay? Or better yet, pray about what you might say. God will give the words and the courage. But remember, the wedding is four days away."

Horrified.

Petrified.

Mortified.

Almost lost in the paralyzing forest of "fieds," the chirping of her cellphone brought him back into the present.

Followed by the sound of "Hello, Sully." He had more to pray about than what to say at the wedding.

CHAPTER FOURTEEN

He slunk down the hall and slipped into his room.

Mom, honest. It wasn't my fault.

Sully didn't see what happened.

Why do you believe him over me?

He paced. Chesty paced step for step alongside him.

"What do you think, boy? Will I be grounded until summer?"

Don't you even want to hear my side of the story?

I think Sully cares more about his reputation than the truth!

"I guess I'll have to take my punishment like a man. It is what it is. Right, Lecty?"

"Ohhh! Take it like a man! Take it like a man!"

"Crazy ole bird!" Jase was thankful for his feathered friend. He believed there were times she actually understood him.

Knowing his mother would storm into his room any moment now, he sat on the edge of his bed and braced himself.

"Jase! Breakfast is on the table. I've got to go—I can't be late my last day of work before the wedding. I'll see you this afternoon. Have a great day!" Her voice carried down the hall, squeezed under the door, and jostled him awake.

He swung his gym shoe clad feet over the side of the bed and rubbed his eyes. Yesterday's jeans, T-shirt, and plaid overshirt smelled like ... well, yesterday.

He wasn't sure how he escaped the wrath of Mom. Maybe she came to banish him to his room for eternity and found him asleep with an angelic glow on his face. Maybe her anger was simmering, and she was taking her time thinking of the perfect punishment. Or perhaps she argued with Sully and told him she didn't believe him.

Whatever the reason, he celebrated the delay in sentencing.

"How about that, Lecty? I get another day of freedom. I'll worry about what's coming later. Maybe today will be better than yesterday. Either way, I will ..."

"Ooooh! Take it like a man! Take it like a man!"

"Crazy old bird!"

"Hey, sleepyhead. Did you lose your brush?" Haley pointed towards Jase's hair.

"Aw, leave him alone. Maybe he's trying out a new look to go with his bad boy self." Steve gave a toothy grin.

"What did your mom do to you?" Deirdre's voice taunted. "I'm sure she's not happy about the Table of Shame."

"Very funny. Everyone is a comedian. My hair is fine. And bad boy? Hardly." Jase made a sweeping motion with his hand as he spoke. "You don't need to worry yourself over my mom or what she did."

"We will miss you during lunch, little buddy. Don't worry, though, we won't let Harrison take your place while you're making nice with Andrew the Giant."

Jase didn't respond to Steve. He wondered why his best friend enjoyed picking on him. He wondered why Deirdre seemed excited about his troubles.

And he wondered why Haley blushed and looked away when Steve mentioned Austin Justin Harry Harrison's name.

CHAPTER FIFTEEN

The Table of Shame.

Jase never imagined he would be seated here. Kids who sat at this table were ... well, they were rule breakers and roughnecks. Troublemakers and rebels.

None of those words described Jase. He considered himself a rule keeper. Someone who looked out for the underdog. One of the good guys.

And yet, here he sat.

“Look, I’m not expecting to be friends with you by the end of this week or ever for that matter.” Andrew didn’t even look at him.

“Fine with me.” Jase wanted to do his time and be done with it.

“Maybe next time, you’ll mind your own business.”

Jase looked at his classmates, the good kids who were seated in their usual spots.

“Or maybe next time, you’ll understand personal space and keep your hands to yourself. And your mouth. You don’t have to be a jerk all the time.”

Andrew dropped his fork onto his tray and quit chewing. Jase didn’t look but he could feel the heat of the glare.

Jase took another bite of his sloppy joe. “Ya know, I’m not afraid of you. Eat or don’t eat. Hate me or not. Doesn’t matter to me.”

"You've got a lot of guts."

"No, not really. I'm just tired of guys like you doing whatever you want to guys like me."

Jase watched his friends, eating and talking and laughing. Did they even miss him? Seemed like they didn't care he was seated here with Andrew the jerk giant.

"My school back home had better lunches. And every Friday we could by pop from the vending machines in the hall."

"Pop? Harrison, what are you talking about?" Deirdre giggled.

"Yeah, Pop is what we call our grandad." Danny giggled as well.

"You know, soda. We could buy soda pop."

"You really are a strange kid, no offense." Steve drank the rest of his milk and crushed the carton.

"What makes you think I'm the strange one? Maybe it's you guys. You say weird stuff. And you talk funny." Harrison's posture improved as he spoke.

"Wait. What? *We* talk funny?"

"Ya, you betcha, you do."

"Uh, naw. Did you hear yourself? 'Ya, you betcha.' *That's* funny talk." Steve's voice raised in excitement over a point made.

"Jase was right." Harrison didn't raise his voice. He spoke and he ate.

"Right about what?" Haley finally spoke.

"Never mind. Forget it." Harrison took another bite.

"We don't play like that at this table. You started it. Now finish it. Right about what?" This time Steve spoke low and slow.

Danny, Deirdre, and Haley stopped eating and waited. Without another word.

"Well ..."

Harrison took another bite.

"He said you ..." And he nodded toward Steve.

"... are not the sharpest knife in the drawer. Not the brightest bulb. A few fries short of a happy meal." And with that, Harrison looked up and smiled.

No one smiled back.

"You don't know what you're talking about." Steve's cheeks flushed red.

"You asked and I told ya. Jase said you're really just a dumb jock."

Steve picked up his tray and walked out of the cafeteria. Right past the Table of Shame.

"What you just did was mean, Harrison." Haley's voice dripped with disgust.

"Yeah. Super mean." Deirdre echoed.

"Why ask me to finish what I was saying if you didn't want to hear it?" Harrison stood and picked up his tray. "Next time don't ask."

Harrison stopped at the Table of Shame on his way out.

"Hey. Thanks again for sticking up for me. Too bad your friends don't appreciate you as much as much as I do." He looked from Jase to Andrew and back at Jase. "Okay, then. See ya later."

Danny scratched his head. "Do you believe him?"

"I'm confused. And I don't get confused." Deirdre placed her hands on her cheeks.

"I don't know. That doesn't sound like something Jase would say. But why would Harrison lie?" Haley's stomach sunk into her shoes.

CHAPTER SIXTEEN

Jase wondered how Mr. Tims managed to get to 624 Juniper Street before he did. Of course, it didn't matter because there he sat.

In his truck.

Waiting.

Shouldn't a boy be allowed a few minutes at home after school without discipline or correction or lectures?

"Mom doesn't get home today until after five."

"You and I need to talk."

"Mr. Tims, I didn't start the fight with Andrew. You didn't—"

"I'm not here to discuss what happened. I want you to know why I haven't told your mom. She's nervous about the wedding, and she has enough on her. Let's agree we need to do whatever we can to make Saturday a great day for her."

"I don't plan on causing any trouble."

"Jase, I hope you know I meant everything I've said about you and your mom. I am going to take good care of both of you. And I have every intention of being the teacher you've known me to be since the beginning of the year. Marrying your mom doesn't change anything. Well, at least I can say it doesn't change *me*."

Jase didn't know where Mr. Tims was going with this conversation. What did he mean 'at least it doesn't change me'? One thing was sure, he wasn't in the mood to argue. He did agree his mom deserved a great wedding. He knew he wouldn't do anything to spoil her day.

"Are you listening, Jase?"

"Yes, sir."

"Whatever set you off with Andrew doesn't matter right now. Try to show some self-control. For your mom."

"But—"

"Stop. Self-control. For your mom."

"Yes, sir."

"Please give this to your mom, and tell her I am sorry I couldn't stay to see her." He handed Jase an envelope.

Mr. Tims started his truck and backed out of the driveway. Jase nodded his goodbye and watched the truck leave.

Wow, okay. What just happened? Self-control? I thought I've always had self-control. At least he hasn't changed. Was he saying I'm the one who has changed?

He tried not to think about the conversation again. But Mr. Tims's words continued to ring in his head.

He had questions that needed answers.

Why didn't Mr. Tims listen to his side of what happened with Andrew?

What did he mean when he said Jase needed self-control?

And did Austin Justin Harry Harrison really say the gang doesn't appreciate him?

He placed the envelope on the kitchen table before heading to his room to retrieve his cellphone. Chesty followed, barking all the while.

Jase: Hey

He pulled his literature book from his backpack and sat it on his desk.

Jase: Hellllooooooo

He tossed a piece of dried fruit to Lecty and checked her water dish.

Jase: Hey. S'up?

"Are you ready to go outside? Let's go!" Chesty raced down the hall after him.

Jase sat down on the steps while Chesty explored the backyard.

Jase: Hey! Are you okay?

Steve: I'm fine. Just searching for my missing fries.

Jase: Huh?

But Steve didn't text back.

CHAPTER SEVENTEEN

"Hey, what happened last night?" Jase found Steve at the locker before homeroom.

"Nothing happened."

"I texted you. Is your phone working?"

"Duh, I dunno, Jase. Maybe I should get someone to show me how to check to be sure." Steve grabbed his books and walked away.

"Hey. Hey! What's that about?" Jase yelled after him, but Steve kept walking.

Jase closed their shared locker and checked the time. He had a few minutes before the bell would ring.

He wove through the crowded hall to find Haley. Surely, she would know what happened to make Steve act weird.

He turned the corner, eyes searching down the hall. He saw the back of Haley's head and opened his mouth to call out her name.

But there, next to her, stood Harrison.

Jase pivoted on the ball of his foot, making a quick U-turn. He slipped back and peered around the corner.

His locker isn't even in this hall. What's he doing? And what am I doing? I have no reason to hide from them.

He ran his hand through his hair, straightened his T-shirt, and finished the trek to Haley.

"Hey, what's up?" His voice lacked the confidence he usually projected.

"Not much. Just getting to class. What about you?" She adjusted her glasses.

"Uh ... well ..." Jase shot a glance at Harrison. "Me neither. I mean, me too. Just going to class."

"Are you okay? You're acting kinda weird."

"I thought *I* was the weird one." Harrison finally spoke.

"I'm fine. Just ... ah ... looking for Steve. Have you seen him?" Jase ignored Harrison.

"Saw him on the bus this morning. Where were you?"

"Oh, uh ... rode in with my mom. Overslept. Was Steve okay? Or was he, you know, in a mood?"

"I don't know. I barely made it to the bus stop in time and we really didn't speak. Are you sure you're okay?"

"Yeah, you really *are* the weird one today." Harrison spoke a bit louder this time.

"I said I'm okay. Gotta go. See ya later." Jase ignored Harrison a second time.

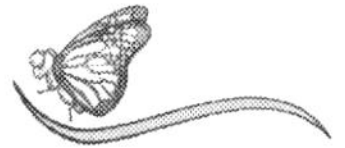

She poured herself a cup of black coffee, ready to enjoy a quiet morning before giving her attention to the list of things to do before the wedding day.

She examined the envelope on the kitchen table. Printed on the front in Sully's handwriting: JUST AN IDEA. LET ME KNOW WHAT YOU THINK.

She sipped her coffee and pulled a brochure from the envelope. The cover boasted of a beautiful beach of white sand and crystal, aqua-blue waters. A trip to the Caribbean.

Tucked in the brochure was a scrap of paper and scribbled on it were the words "choose the dates, and I'll buy the tickets. You deserve a few days away."

Oh my, this looks beautiful. And tempting. But what about Jase?

CHAPTER EIGHTEEN

"I saw you have a new seat in the cafeteria. What happened? Did you have a bad day?" Mr. Houston stopped Jase as he walked into homeroom.

"Just tried to do the right thing, and Mr. Tims gave me trouble for it, that's all."

"I don't know. Mr. Tims doesn't usually step in when a student is doing the right thing."

"Mr. Houston, I don't think it matters. No one wants to hear what happened anyway."

"Give me a try."

"Andrew was messing with the new kid, Austin ... uh, Harrison. I told him to back off and he didn't."

"What's the rest of the story?"

"He pointed his finger at me, and he flicked my nose. He went too far. So, I shoved him."

"Well, son, I can't say I blame you. But I'm not saying you did the right thing, either. Have you thought of a better way?"

"No. To be honest I haven't thought about it at all. I'm trying to get through the next couple of days."

"Sometimes you need to ignore the big mouths in the world. They lose steam when no one takes the bait."

"Yeah. I guess." Jase walked to his desk as the bell rang.

He decided to keep his nose clean for the day or at least give it his best shot. He remembered the first time his mother made the statement before he left for school one morning. He thought it was a disgusting thing to say, but she explained she meant to stay out of trouble. Mind his own business. He also decided he would put his nose to the grindstone. After all, if a guy is going to keep his nose clean, he might as well make good use of it.

So today. Minding his own business was exactly what he would do. And focus on the task at hand.

He found it surprisingly easy to stick to his studies when he made the choice to. When thoughts of Austin Justin Harry Harrison crept in, he simply reread the last paragraph in chapter 48 of his science textbook. If he happened to wonder why Steve was acting weird, he rechecked his answers on the worksheet he'd just completed. And each moment of doubt over how life was changing and what the coming wedding might mean simply led him to study the definitions of the vocabulary list in from of him.

He knew he could do this. Science class down, three more classes to go.

And lunch.

With Andrew the Crude.

And the Table of Shame.

He entered literature class, and in keeping with a spotless nose, sat at his desk without speaking to anyone.

Enter Harrison.

"Hey, Jase. Did you ever find Steve?"

"No. Went to class instead." *Please go away. You're making my nose dirty.*

"Oh, well. If I see him, I'll tell him you're looking for him."

"K. Thanks." *Now go sit down.*

Harrison paused, and Jase kept busy organizing his textbook and last night's homework on his desktop. He pulled an ink pen from the side pocket of his backpack.

This is how a guy puts his clean nose to the grindstone.

Harrison shrugged and went to his desk.

Victory.

"I'm excited about our next adventure! I've given much thought to the exercise we will begin today and conclude next week." Jase had never heard Miss Teal say a single word in frustration or in any tone other than a patient one until today.

She turned the smartboard on to reveal a list of twenty-five book titles.

"There is much to learn when you must work with others. I will assign you to groups of three. Together, you will choose a book to read. Each person from the group will be responsible for one of the following: illustrate one scene on a poster board, write an alternate ending, or recite a passage from memory. Of course, you will have to work this out among yourselves."

A mix of groans and cheers followed Miss Teal's announcement. Jase exhaled and dropped his forehead to his desk with a loud thud.

"Jase? Are you okay?" Sincerity always in her voice.

Snickers, giggles, and smirks rolled around the room.

He sat up straight and nodded.

Please, Miss Teal. Please do not put me with the new kid.

"Your groups are as follows ..."

Groups. Not a great way to mind my own business.

Jase's mind swirled out of control as the dam burst, and the flood of thoughts he held at bay in first period rushed in like a tsunami. Miss Teal's soft voice was now under water, muffled and fuzzy.

Until.

She said.
"Jase Freeman ..."
What?
"Madeline Jones ..."
And?
"Jessie Silver."
YES!
"Oh. Wait. No, I'm sorry. My mistake ..."
Huh?
"Harrison Peterson."

CHAPTER NINETEEN

Noooooooooooo!

He looked over his shoulder at Harry. Harry grinned and gave two thumbs up. Jase gave a half smile and an unenthused single thumb up.

"There's no time like the present. Get with your fellow group members and choose a title. First come, first serve to the bookshelf. Choose quickly and wisely. Your first choice might be gone if you spend too much time debating."

Madeline's desk sat strategically between Jase's and Harrison's. So, they met in the middle.

Madeline spoke as soon as the boys pulled their chairs to her desk.

"Okay. I want an "A" on this project. So, no slacking. I've already read most of the books on the list. You guys can choose. Ready? Go!" She folded her hands in front of her after flipping her long, curly, red hair over her shoulder.

"I choose *Wonder*." Harrison spoke up before Jase had a chance.

Jase briefly studied the list.

"Mmm, Harry Potter books are too big to read in a week and still have time to finish the rest of the assignment. I choose *Tuck Everlasting*."

"Okay. *The Book Thief*, it is." Madeline retrieved three copies of the book.

Harrison and Jase gave each other confused, what-just-happened stares.

"Today is Thursday. Can you finish reading by Monday morning? We can meet in the library before school Monday to decide who will be responsible for the three parts of the assignment."

"This is supposed to be a group project. Who put *you* in charge?" Jase knew he risked getting his nose dirty, but the question needed to be asked.

"Someone has to take charge. Might as well be me." Her tone didn't have a bossy air about it, even though she clearly took charge of this small group.

"Okay. I give." He retreated. Better to conform and finish the day in the safe cocoon of his own business.

"I guess I agree." Harrison's tone, reluctant and unsure.

"See you Monday morning in the library. Can you be here by 7:30?" Madeline pushed and didn't wait for answers. "Good then. Now go. Get busy. You have a book to read."

Jase didn't know what happened or how he lost complete control so quickly. One thing was certain, he no longer wondered about Steve or Mr. Tims or weddings and stepdads.

He looked at Austin Justin Harry Harrison's face and wondered. What would it be ...

Harrison Peterson.

In the library.

With a poster board?

And is it possible for a guy to keep his nose clean when forced to work with Harry, read a book he wasn't interested in, attend his mother's wedding, and figure out what's going on with his best friend ... all in the same weekend?

CHAPTER TWENTY

Lime gelatin. And a corndog. And soggy fries.

Who exactly chooses the menu? The corndog isn't too bad. But seriously. Lime gelatin?

Jase stared at his lunch tray and pondered his reality.

Lime gelatin and Andrew the Grouch-tastic.

Like an instant replay from the day before, the two picked at and ate their lunches without the benefit of friendly conversation.

Well. Almost.

Jase glanced over at Andrew the Crude, and for the first time, noticed his shirt was faded and his jeans had several holes in them. Not the rips over the knees meant to be cool kind of holes. More like these jeans were worn by three older brothers before making it to Andrew kind of holes.

Andrew's bangs were long enough to cover his eyes when he failed to brush them over to one side.

He opened his mouth and the words spilled out.

"I'm an only child. You have any sisters or brothers?"

Andrew shook his tray and watched the gelatin jiggle.

Why can't I just keep my nose clean?

"What's it to you?"

"I dunno. I guess I thought ... we have to eat together, we might as well talk. Maybe the time will pass faster."

"I already told you I don't need no new friend."

Jase shrugged and took another bite of his corndog.

"Five."

"What?"

"I have five brothers. I'm the baby. So, there's six of us."

"Wow. Bet there's never a dull minute at your house."

"What's that supposed to mean?" Andrew tossed his head so his brown bangs piled over to one side. His green eyes were all squinty and fierce looking. Jase expected a laser beam to shoot out at any moment and fry him to a crisp.

"Nothing. Nothing at all. I just meant ... well, my house is boring. It's just me and my dog and a bird. And my mom ... so, yeah. There's no one to horse around with or play video games."

"I wouldn't mind trying a couple days of quiet. We fight. A lot."

"Oh." Jase considered trying a bite of the wiggly jiggly green stuff to keep his mouth shut. Considered and denied.

"What's his name?"

"Who? I don't have a brother."

"The dog."

"Chesty. He's named after a Marine Corps hero."

"Does he play fetch? I seen dogs on TV play fetch. Looks fun."

"Nah. He looks at me like I'm crazy when I've tried to teach him."

"Still. I bet it's fun having a dog."

Jase was beginning to see Andrew in a whole new light. He wasn't Andrew the Crude or the Terrible. Maybe he was Andrew the Lonely. Or Andrew the Warrior. Maybe he learned all his insults from his older brothers. Maybe he picked on Harry because he wanted to be the one doing the picking instead of being on the receiving end.

"Yeah, it is. He's like a best friend."

As if they had not spoken a word, they both went back to eating. Andrew ate his soggy fries. He even ate the green stuff.

"Can you bring a picture? Of your dog?"

"I think I can find one. Sure. Yeah."

"See ya tomorrow." And Andrew the Misunderstood picked up his tray and left.

Jase picked at the fries and considered eating one. He couldn't do it. Not because the fry was soggy. No.

No. His appetite walked out of the cafeteria with Andrew. Hunger was replaced with guilt. Guilt for complaining about his life being hard. Guilt over thinking his life wasn't fair.

He wondered if his nose was still clean.

CHAPTER TWENTY-ONE

Sometimes a person's mind simply takes a trip to a worry-free place ... or two ... or more.

An amusement park is fun. The rollercoaster creeping to the peak and dropping the riders to near death right before spinning them upside down. He closed his eyes and focused on the thrill of the ride. Disorientation. Nausea. Blinded by centrifugal force. The worst part—the fun is over seemingly seconds after it begins.

The score is tied. Three seconds remain on the clock. The crowds representing both schools are up on their feet, shouting, clapping, cheering. Jase hears the crowd yelling "Pass the ball to Freeman! Pass it to Freeman!" He throws his hands up and catches the basketball, briefly pivoting before taking the shot. Nothing but net! Once again, Jase Freeman brings victory!

A cool breeze brushes over him as he walks through the woods. Sticks and leaves crunch and crackle beneath his feet. He looks up at the canopy above, formed by the limbs of trees as they stretch toward each other. The sight reminds him of the pictures he's seen of an arch of sabers formed by two lines of Marines in dress blues, standing at attention with swords drawn and held high, cutting edge up forming an arch for honored guests to pass through. The trees and critters, the sky and breeze—they remind him there is Someone far greater than he. They almost shout the existence of God. He exhales.

Trouble in the Halls

"Jase, please share your answer to number fourteen."

Snapping back to the classroom at the sound of his name, and well, the sound of the laughter of his classmates.

"Uh ... um ... sir?"

"Number fourteen. We worked even numbers through twelve together. You should be able to share your work."

The tops of his ears grew hot as the fire of embarrassment engulfed them. The deep red color made its way downward and did not stop at his earlobes. No. The redness traveled to his neck and turned blotchy.

There he sat. In algebra with a blotchy neck and bright red-hot ears, all eyes on him, the teacher tap, tap, tapping his pencil on his desk as everyone waits for an answer.

And no answer came.

The tap, tap, tapping stopped, and the air left the room.

"Jase, you can complete the rest of the even numbers of this chapter for homework tonight. Anyone else thinking of daydreaming the class away?"

He sat in stunned disbelief.

How is this fair?

Are you kidding me?

What happens if I don't do it?

If only he could transport himself out of this room. He'd gladly be banished to the woods or sentenced to an endless coaster ride in exchange for too many algebra equations to solve and a teacher who would soon become his stepdad.

This.

This is not how a guy keeps his nose clean.

CHAPTER TWENTY-TWO

"One more day. Just one more day till the weekend." Haley's cheery outlook sometimes annoyed Jase beyond words.

"Uh-huh. And one more day till the wedding of the century." He would prefer to ride home in silence, but when Haley was around, silence didn't happen.

"I'm so excited! I have a dress picked out, and I know how I will wear my hair. I'm going to wear my sparkly heels and ..." She quit speaking when he grunted at the word sparkly.

"I wish I could fast forward all the way to spring break. I think I'll ask my mom if I can go to Pop and Juju's."

"I'm sorry you are dreading the wedding. I guess I thought you'd be happy for your mom. And you could do a lot worse for a stepdad. Mr. Tims is one of the good guys. Maybe you're focusing on yourself a little too much. Just saying." And with that, she moved to another seat for the remaining bus ride to Juniper Street.

She's right, of course. Why does she always have to be right?

He assessed the day. He began determined to keep his nose clean and ended with a group project with Austin Justin Harry Harrison and Madeline the Mighty. The Table of Shame opened his eyes to what Andrew's life might be like and ... well ... guilt is no fun. Don't forget extra algebra homework all because he let his mind take a stress-relieving detour. Or two. Or three.

An extra helping of guilt piled on by Haley's truthful self could not have been less welcomed.

He gritted his teeth and watched the snow flurries swirl through the air. He battled within and wondered why he spent too much time focusing on himself and not enough time being happy for his mom.

He could do better.

He *would* do better.

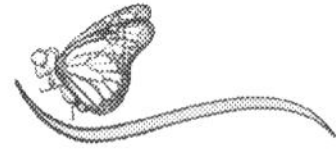

He dropped his backpack at the door and called out for his mom.

"I'm in the kitchen."

"Hey. Did you get a lot done today? What can I do to help?"

"Aw! Thank you, Son. It's been a productive day. I think I'm ready."

Jase smiled back at her.

"When will the family get here? Anyone staying here?"

"Aunt Christy will stay here. Pop and Juju, Uncle Caleb, and Grandma Lynny and Grandpa Rocky will stay downtown at the Mountain Laurel Inn. Everyone will be here by tomorrow afternoon."

Jase hugged his mom.

"Wow, what a nice surprise." She stepped back and placed her hand under his chin. "Are you okay?"

"I'm just glad for you. You deserve to be happy. Sully is a good guy. I love you, Mom."

"I love you too. And I'm glad for both of us. It's okay to be happy for yourself, Jase. Your daddy would want you to always remember him and to know who you are and whose you are. You look just like him, you know. And you act like him too." She kissed the top of his head. "Won't be long, and I'll need to stand on a chair to reach you." Her laughter filled the room like the sun when it chases darkness away.

"About my part in the vows. Is there a Scripture verse I can read or something?"

"I think that's a perfect idea. How about if you choose the verses? You can let us know tomorrow night at rehearsal. Deal?"

"Deal. I have a ton of homework, so I better get to it."

He already knew what verse he would read, or actually, he could recite it.

Philippians 1:6.

Perfect.

CHAPTER TWENTY-THREE

He shuddered thinking about the group project and spending quality time with Austin Justin Harry Harrison. He couldn't put his finger on it, but there was just something about the guy that didn't feel right. His gut told him something was off. But Jase wasn't entirely sure he could trust his gut.

"Hey, Lecty. How about you read this book for me and take care of the library meeting next week? There will be extra pineapple in it for you." Jase tossed her a piece of dried fruit. She caught it, and after she ate it, she responded, "Ooooh, no. No! No!"

"I thought you were my friend, ole bird."

"Ooooh, no! No!"

He laughed at his bird's vocabulary and use of the words she had learned.

He pulled *The Book Thief* from his backpack and read a few chapters before supper.

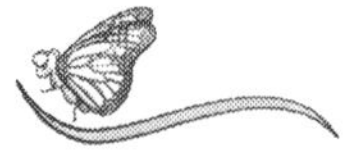

"I think you have a great idea. In fact, how soon can we go?" She twisted her hair around her finger as she spoke into her cellphone.

"I'm a step ahead of you. I've talked with your boss and Pop and Juju. We will leave Saturday evening after the wedding reception and return home Tuesday afternoon. Pop and Juju will stay and take care of Jase while we are away. What do you say?"

"I say yes! I can't believe you took care of everything. What a wonderful time away after all the busyness of holidays and wedding preparations. I can't wait! If someone had told me a year ago I would be this happy ... well, I wouldn't have believed I could ever be half this happy." Janice's voice began to quiver.

"Hey, now. No crying. No tears. Go pack, and I'll see you tomorrow at the rehearsal."

"I love you, Sully."

"I love you too."

His stomach growled and sent him to the kitchen. He had not planned to overhear his mom on the phone. Really, he didn't mean to be in the wrong place at the wrong time. More drama in his day was the last thing he wanted.

Go? Go where? Sully took care of everything? What about me? I suppose this is just a hint of my future. I was in the loop when life was just Mom and me. I guess I'll have to learn to wait to be told what's coming. No say. No vote. I'm not sure I like this.

Grouchiness can arrive like a hawk swooping in on an unsuspecting rat. Did the anger rise from inside him or settle in from the top of his head? Where the mood of doom and gloom came from didn't matter. What mattered was, he was consumed by lack of say. Lack of control.

If someone had told me a year ago I would have no say in my life, I would have laughed. I would have said no. My mom and me are a team.

He didn't feel so hungry any longer. His mom stepped into the kitchen before he could slink out.

"Hey, don't eat anything now. Supper will be here in about ten minutes. Don't spoil your appetite."

“Did you order out? You usually ask me what I want before you order.”

“You were busy with your homework. I ordered pizza. Pepperoni and Italian sausage. Sound good?”

“I guess. Just wish you would have asked me.”

“It’s just pizza. More drama?”

First just pizza. Then you can’t believe he took care of everything, and you’re ready to get away. What will tomorrow be? Gonna send me to boarding school or something?

Appetite.

Spoiled.

CHAPTER TWENTY-FOUR

"Morning. Your light was still on last night when I went to bed. Did you get any sleep?"

"A little. Just had a lot of homework. I think some teachers get sick satisfaction over assigning too much work for a guy to be able to finish and get enough sleep too."

"Just do the best you can, that's all that is asked of you."

"Nothing is asked. I get told." He grabbed an apple and gave his mom a quick hug. "See you this afternoon."

"Nothing is asked ... he gets told?" She repeated his words as he walked out the door.

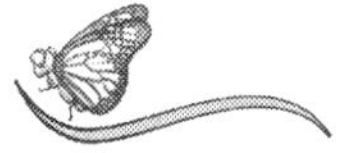

Staying up late the night before didn't stop Jase from getting up early enough to get to the bus stop in time to talk with Steve.

He'd sent Steve several texts last night and never got an answer. Jase was determined to find out why.

Moments after he arrived, Danny and Deirdre walked up, deep in conversation over which illustrated classic was best. They didn't acknowledge Jase, which didn't bother him a bit. He watched and listened as they went back and forth, listing the reasons each one's favorite was the best.

Jase rolled his eyes and looked over his shoulder to see Haley and Steve—they were also deep in conversation as they settled in to wait for the bus.

"I don't know. Looks to me like he's doing just fine. I don't know why you worry about everybody so much." Steve gave Haley his full attention.

"I don't worry. I care. And he just seems ... well ... I don't know. I'm trying to figure out what is going on with him. I haven't seen him hanging out with anyone. Just us at lunch."

"Like I said. You worry too much. He's been at Crumberry Middle School for a week. Give the guy time to figure us out. And seriously. We need time to figure him out." Steve had not spoken to anyone else yet.

"Sup, you two. Are y'all coming to the big wedding tomorrow?"

"Are you kidding? I wouldn't miss it! Remember, I have my dress and heels ready."

"Oh, yeah. Yeah, I remember." Jase tried to smile but instead his mouth went all crookedy. That's what happens when he forced a smile. Crookedy.

Steve shrugged. "I dunno. Haven't decided yet." Did Steve's tone cause the temperature to drop a few degrees or did Jase imagine the chill?

The bus pulled up to the curb, and Jase decided the timing was perfect. What did Steve mean he hadn't decided yet?

A guy's best friend wouldn't think of missing.

Hmm. Key words 'best friend.'

Did he even have a best friend anymore?

Did Crumberry get picked up in the middle of the night and dropped in the Bermuda Triangle?

Or maybe aliens invaded and slipped in under the radar, messing up lives and friendships.

Friendships, illustrated classics, dresses and heels, *The Book Thief* project—those worries won't matter in just a few hours.

Because in a few hours, Pop and Juju would arrive in Crumberry. Who needs a best friend when you have a Pop?

Jase wondered why Steve was acting strange. He wondered why Haley was talking about Austin Justin Harry Harrison again. And he wondered what words of wisdom Pop would have to help him understand how, in less than a week, his world had turned topsy turvy.

CHAPTER TWENTY-FIVE

"He's bigger now. I took this picture at my Pop's farm in Kentucky. I got to go during Christmas break."

"How big will he get?" Andrew held a picture of Chesty.

"I read he will weigh about fifty pounds when he's grown, but he will stay kinda short."

"Is he mean? He looks mean."

"No. He likes everybody he meets. He's a big baby."

Jase and Andrew talked like old friends the last day of their Table of Shame sentence. He wasn't sure what the purpose of the Table of Shame was other than to embarrass those who were exiled there. He decided he had made a new friend, even if they never hung out or anything.

Come Monday, Andrew would go back to his eighth-grade buddies, and Jase would take his place at the table with the gang. Well, he hoped he would. He hoped Steve would be over whatever was bugging him. And he dared hoped Haley would stop acting so interested in the new kid from Canada or Minnesota or wherever.

"Hi, Mr. Tims. May I come in?" Harrison arrived early to algebra.

Mr. Tims nodded and motioned for Harrison to enter.

"Do you ever tutor?"

"I'll be glad to help you, Harrison. What are you struggling with?"

"All the decimal stuff. I asked Jase if he would help me. But ... well ... never mind." Harrison walked to his desk and sat down.

"Jase is a good student. He should be able to help you."

"Well, he wasn't very nice. That's all."

"I'm sorry, Harrison. I'd be glad to help you. I'm sure you'll catch on."

"So, are you going to tell me what's going on, or what?" Jase met Steve at the locker.

Steve closed the locker and paused, giving Jase hopes of an actual conversation.

"Or what." And he walked away.

He watched Steve enter the crowded hall. Watched as he was swallowed up in the sea of students hurrying to class.

Puzzled.

Confused.

And late to algebra.

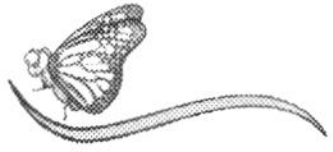

He slipped into class, placed his homework on Mr. Tims's desk and slunk into his seat.

"Glad you could make it, Jase." Mr. Tims didn't smile. In fact, he frowned. A real furrowed brow, corners of his mouth turned down frown. At Jase.

"I'm sorry I'm late."

"Just don't do it again."

And there it was. The now familiar warmth of blood rushing to his ears and down into his neck. How long before he would earn the nickname of Blotchy Boy or maybe just plain Red?

"Yes, sir."

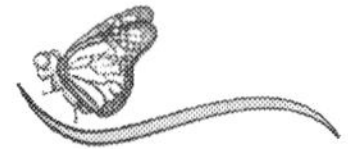

"Coach K, do you have Jase Freeman in class?" The question came from the intercom in the corner of the gym.

"Yes, ma'am. He's here."

"Send him to the office, please."

"You heard her, Jase."

He stepped into the hall outside the gym and waited. Waited for the reason to come to him.

What had he done now? How did he mess up bad enough to be summoned to the office and not have a clue what he did?

He put one foot in front of the other and began the long walk of solitude.

Head held high.

Blotchy Boy—on his way to the office.

CHAPTER TWENTY-SIX

"Wow! What happened to you?"

"What are you doing in the hall, Harrison? And what do you mean what happened to me?"

"Needed to go to my locker. Where are you going?"

"Office."

"Sick?"

"No."

"Oh. I figured you're not well. I mean. Your neck and all."

"What's wrong with my neck?"

"It's all rashy-lookin'. Red and splotchy."

"I'm fine."

A strange whistly sound came out of Harrison's mouth. "Well, what did you do this time?"

"I don't even know. Just got paged to go."

"You were a poet and didn't even know it." Harrison chuckled.

"Huh?"

"Never mind. Well, hope you're not in a lot of trouble. And remember. No matter what, at least it's not a poke in ..."

"I know, I know. My eye with a sharp stick. You should stop saying that."

"Why? Because you guys never heard it before? I can say what I want."

"Whatever. Don't say I never tried to help you."

They parted ways.

Well.

Almost.

"Hey, Jase?" Harrison used a hushed tone.

"Yeah?"

"Probably not my business, but Steve laughed at you today at lunch. He said if you don't start growing, you're always going to look like a toddler. I told him to stop making fun of you, but he made a few more short jokes anyway."

"You're right. Not your business."

And they parted ways. This time for sure.

His jaws tightened and his steps pounded, each step heavier than the one before as he finished his trek to the office.

What's going on? Short jokes? In front of Austin Justin Harry Harrison? Seriously? Good thing today is Friday. There's no telling where I'd end up if I had one more day in the week.

Andrew stepped from around the corner.

He'd heard every word.

A friendship had formed at the Table of Shame.

And Andrew the Detective was sure he smelled trouble at Crumberry Middle School.

Jase took a deep breath and exhaled, imagining all the blotchy redness dissipating through his breath. Head held high, shoulders back, and chin out he opened the office door ready to face Principal Drew for the second time this week.

CHAPTER TWENTY-SEVEN

"Pop?" Best. Principal's office. Visit. Ever. "I'm so glad to see you. You have no idea."

Being with Pop was like wearing your most comfortable shoes or sitting in your favorite chair. Being near him brought a you-don't-need-to-worry-about-a-thing kind of comfortable, safe feeling.

"Nice meeting you, Principal Drew. Thank you for everything you do for my grandson and the other kids." Pop extended his right hand to Principal Drew.

"A pleasure to meet you. You can be proud of Jase. I'm sure he will succeed at whatever he sets his mind to."

Jase was more ready than anyone could have known to get out of CMS and start the weekend. Even a weekend when he would have to dress up and watch his mom marry his algebra teacher.

The surprise of seeing Pop and skipping the bus ride home was a bonus. The excitement of seeing Juju and Uncle Caleb brought a surge of energy. He would get home and hug Juju and relax in the don't-worry-about-a-thing feeling.

"Are you ready for tonight and tomorrow? Pretty big weekend ahead for everyone."

"This weekend is the easy part."

"Hmm, good point. Are you ready for life after this weekend?"

"I don't know, Pop. I guess I have to be."

"I'm going to tell you what my dad told me when I had to deal with experiences I wasn't exactly excited to face. He told me many times to 'go with the flow and roll with the punches.'"

"Huh? I'm not expecting to get punched anytime soon."

"Not a literal punch. When life takes turns and changes, and you're not sure what's coming next, you learn to take experiences minute by minute. When you face unexpected challenges, those difficulties can feel like a punch in the gut. Roll with the punches just means you don't fight back. You do what you need to do to make the best of whatever circumstance you find yourself living."

"I'll try to remember."

Pop parked his truck in front of the house. Jase looked at all the vehicles in the driveway and street. Everyone had arrived.

Rocky, Grandma Lynny, and Aunt Christy.

Pop, Juju, and Uncle Caleb.

He opened the front door for Pop and hurried in behind him. What followed was a burst of laughter and hugs and exclamations of happiness. Jase had never experienced so much family in one room at one time.

After he greeted everyone, he found an unoccupied corner and squished himself in so he could watch and listen to the adults catch up with one another. About an hour later, he slipped into his room for a little bit of quiet.

"Lecty, what do you think, girl? Rocky and Grandma Lynny and Pop and Juju. All here at the same time!"

"Ohhh! Rawk! At the same time! At the same time!"

Chesty barked his approval.

Jase sat at his desk and picked up the picture of his dad. He wished he could talk with him. Hear his dad say everything would be okay.

"I miss you. I don't think I'm ready for this. But will I ever be ready? If I could, I'd snap my fingers or wish on a star and have you back here where you belong. Sully is a nice guy, but he will never be you."

A knock at the door brought Jase back to the reality.

"Hey, Son, hiding out from all the excitement?"

"Just for a few minutes."

"You okay?" She nodded toward the picture he still held in his hands.

"Yeah, I think so. It's just ..."

"Come sit by me," she said as she sat on his bed. "We've been through a lot, you and me. You are the best son on the planet, and we will always be a team. Don't feel guilty when you have mixed emotions about how our lives are changing. And know—accepting Sully doesn't change your love for your dad."

"Thanks, Mom. We're going to be okay."

"We're going to be better than okay. We are going to trust God to help us become a family. We need to leave for the church soon. Will you be ready?"

"Yes, ma'am. I'm hungry, though. When do we eat?"

"We'll all go to Palmisano's Pizza after rehearsal. Sound good?"

"Sounds great!"

"Oh, by the way. What would you think if I told you Pop and Juju are going to stay a couple of days and take care of you while Sully and I go on a short honeymoon?"

"Cool! I couldn't be in better hands."

She hugged him before leaving his room.

He wondered if having Pop and Juju here would help him get ready for life with a stepdad. He wondered if Sully would ever get off his case at school. And he wondered what better than okay would be like.

CHAPTER TWENTY-EIGHT

He hung out in the back of the church.

Watching.

Listening.

Experiencing the strange moments he never imagined would actually happen.

A guy can spend hours imagining his dad showing up at school, or walking in the door late one evening, or even calling early one morning to say he would see them soon. He had perfected the home movie playing over and over again in his mind, sometimes in his sleep and often while he stared at the ceiling above his bed, too tired to sleep. How does this weekend change the movie?

Wedding practice.

His mother's laughter.

Happiness everywhere.

Now that everyone, including Jase, knew where to stand and when, what to say and when, where to go and when, Pastor Jim prayed.

He asked God to bless the new family, strengthen love and commitment, help them all to forgive misunderstandings and learn to listen.

And much to Jase's surprise, Pastor prayed for him. He asked God to keep every memory of his dad alive and real, to help Jase adjust to this new adventure and to make room in Jase's heart for Sully.

Pastor said amen, and Jase opened his eyes. Sniffles and smiles, giggles and tears. This wedding stuff was emotion soup.

"Hey, I was promised pizza. Let's eat!"

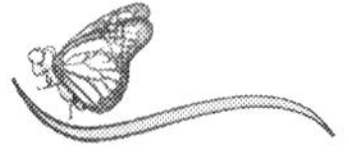

Jase was sure the reward of Palmisano's Pizza made wedding practice bearable. A guy can easily sit at the end of a long table full of family members talking about stuff he didn't want to know, as long as he could eat as much pizza as he wanted.

The buffet was loaded with everything he often called his favorites. What a great distraction! Too many slices later, he slowed down and paid attention to the people at the table.

Mom.

Eyes all happy looking, and her smile—well, her smile ruled the room.

Sully.

Had Sully been a part of their lives forever? Sure seemed as if he had always been here. Uncle Caleb sat next to him. Instant friendship. They kind of reminded Jase of a grown-up version of him and Steve.

Steve. Wonder what Steve's doing tonight. Hope he comes to the wedding tomorrow. Maybe we can figure out what happened to wreck our friendship.

Pop and Juju sat next to Uncle Caleb. Coolest grandparents ever. Biscuit-baking, treehouse-building, advice-giving, story-telling grandparents. The best part of the visit was they will stay a few days longer, and he would get them all to himself. Juju reached over and patted Pop's hand before sipping her sweet tea.

Grandma Lynny wore the same smile his mom had draped across her face. A something more than happy kind of smile. A grateful smile. A content kind of smile. And her smile beamed like a flashlight toward Rocky. The grandfather he thought he would never know.

Aunt Christy—Aunt Crispy as he used to call her. One of the most annoying but fun adults ever in the history of aunts. His mom's best friend. And if he ever needed one, an adult who always had his back.

"I have an announcement to make." Sully cleared his throat. "More good news. Well, I think it's good anyway."

He paused.

Family members, one by one, stopped chewing. Swallowed. A few sipped their tea. Everyone stared.

"I received a text on the way over from the church ..."

Okay? Why the drama? Just say it already.

"I would have told you all sooner, but I wasn't sure everything would fall into place."

"Sully, just say it. What's the news?" Mom's voice crawled with frustration.

"My parents will arrive in town tomorrow morning and will be here for the celebration."

Huh? Another set of grandparents?

Sully had never mentioned his parents. Jase had never asked. He figured he had enough to keep track of and worry about, and whatever story was to be told concerning the Tims family could wait.

An awkward hush moved over the table from one end to the other. Jase heard "oh, how wonderful" and "I can't wait to meet them."

He watched his mom, though. She didn't say anything. She looked down at her plate and rearranged two slices of half-eaten pizza. He wished he could know her thoughts. Because they were Team Freeman, and he knew her—well, he knew she wasn't happy about the announcement. But, why? That he did not know.

In a matter of seconds, the family members around the table went back to their jabber-jawing, and the air of celebration swept back in.

He stopped eating long enough to think about how God had taken care of them. He thought a thankful prayer. Not just for everything God was doing, but also because he recognized all this was special. He might not have chosen the path, but not only did God know the path, he walked the path ahead of them, alongside, and behind. And whatever was going on in his mom's thoughts, well, God knew, and God would take care of her. Jase didn't doubt this. All he had to do was look back and count the ways God had already taken care of them.

The verse he would recite at the wedding tomorrow described their family. And for Jase, knowing God is trustworthy makes all the difference in the best of days and the worst.

CHAPTER TWENTY-NINE

He stood where he was told to stand. And he didn't tug at the collar and tie threatening to choke him to death.

My lips are turning blue. I'm sure they are blue. And is it hot in here? I think the temperature is rising.

There he stood. In the front. Not far from his mom. His turn to speak inched ever near.

"Janice Freeman, do you take this man ..."

Everything is going to be okay."

"I do."

"Sullivan Tims, do you take this woman ..."

Just breathe, Jase. Deep and slow. Breathe in. Breathe out.

"I do."

Rings. Two rings exchanged. More smiles.

"Jase, I understand you have a word to share." Pastor Jim motioned for Jase to begin.

He swallowed. His tongue stuck to the roof of his mouth and the collar squeezed a little tighter.

"Mom, you and Dad always taught me to remember who I am and whose I am. You show me what it means to trust God. Sully, I welcome you to our family. Philippians 1:6 is now our family verse. It goes like this, 'being confident of this very thing, that he who has begun a good work in you ... well, in us ... will complete it until the day of Christ Jesus.'"

He stepped back to his standing spot. Both grandma's sniffled, and Aunt Christy dabbed a tissue to the corner of her eye.

He glanced at the crowd of guests. He didn't know half the people there.

I wonder where they are. Mr. and Mrs. Tims. Are they the couple in the back? Could the round lady with glasses wearing a purple hat be Sully's mom? And the bald man next to her, wearing a frown. Could it be?

"You may kiss your bride."

Wait. What? Ew.

"Ladies and gentlemen, I present to you Sullivan and Janice Tims."

Cheers and applause followed, so loud Pastor Jim had to use a microphone to invite everyone to the reception in fellowship hall.

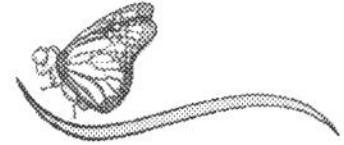

They hugged and slapped each other on the back. Sully's dad stepped aside, and Sully hugged his mother.

"I can't believe you made it! Jase, come here!" Sully waved at Jase. "Mom, Dad, meet Jase. Jase, say hello to Don and Margo Tims."

"We've heard you are an impressive young man." Her voice barely above a whisper, Sully's mom smiled and extended her hand. Her short, brown hair curled around her face and Jase imagined, even in hurricane force winds, the hair would have stayed in place.

"Hello. Nice to meet you."

"She's right. Sully told us all about you." The tall, thin man reached for Jase's hand and shook it enthusiastically. He wore a polka dot bow tie, almost distracting Jase from the man's mustache with whirly, swirly curls at each end.

Jase looked at the lady's hair and the man's mustache. His amazement grew as his gaze lingered, and he tried to figure out what kind of glue they must have used. He wished a gust of air would blow through the fellowship hall so he could see for himself if either the 'stache or hairdo would show signs of life.

The tall, thin man with the curly 'stache folded his arms across his chest. The sweet woman next to him placed her hand in the crook of his elbow. They wore smiles almost as stiff as their hair.

Awkward.

Pause.

"I'm glad you're hair ... uh, uh, here. Glad to meet you."

"Sully, old man! You did it!" Coach K's booming voice provided the perfect escape for Jase. He took advantage of the introductions and slipped into the crowd.

He weaved and dodged and wondered. They'd heard all about him. Why had Sully not told him about this odd-looking pair he called Dad and Mom?

"Jase! Wasn't it just dreamy? The flowers, the lights, the music. Just dreamy." Haley placed her hands over her heart and looked up as if she were watching a replay.

Jase curled his lip and wrinkled his nose.

Haley gazed in disbelief at his scrunched expression. "What? You mean you don't think it was dreamy?"

"Last I checked, boys don't use the word dreamy."

"Why do boys always have to be so droll?"

"Dreamy? Droll? You've been watching old movies again, haven't you? Or too many Hallmark Christmas specials."

"Would you rather I ask why boys are stupid? How do you even know about Hallmark movies?"

"I live with my mom, remember? And they are all the same, but she watches them with a tissue in her hand as if each one has a different storyline. I'm not stupid, but the movies sure are."

"Oh, Jase. You're hopeless."

"Nah, just keepin' it real. I'm going to get a slice of cake. Real cake. No dreams necessary."

She watched him walk away. She shrugged and looked for someone who would understand just how dreamy the day had been.

Jase, you look super cute in your wedding clothes. Actually, you're kind of dreamy too.

CHAPTER THIRTY

Jase reached for the largest slice of wedding cake on the table. He found a corner of the small fellowship hall and sat down to eat in peace.

He watched his mom and Mr. Tims ... uh, Sully, shake hands with guests and smile as they greeted the well-wishers. He thought of how often he heard his mom say she wanted a small wedding but soon added another name to the guest list.

He tugged at his collar and wondered if anyone would notice if he loosened this death grip before he lost too much oxygen to his brain.

He took a large bite of cake and looked up to see Haley talking to Deirdre. They both had their hands on their hearts.

Girls.

He weaved and dodged through the mass of wedding guests, searching for Steve. He stood on his toes to try to look above the crowd. He hoped to hear Steve's voice booming an obnoxious Steve-ism.

Weaving and dodging is exhausting, and the best treatment for running out of energy is cake, right? Are two slices of cake too many? Nah.

"Deirdre agrees with me." Haley smiled a 'dreamy' smile.

"Yeah. I do. I really do."

"Good. I'm glad you found someone to talk dreams with. Hey, have you seen Steve?"

Haley and Deirdre stared at Jase and then each other. Deirdre looked at her feet.

"What? Where's Steve?"

"We hoped you'd be so busy you wouldn't notice or ask." Haley reached over and put her hand on his arm.

"Okay?"

"Steve is home."

"So, he didn't want to come to a wedding. Can't blame the guy."

"Well ... okay. Harrison is at Steve's. They are gaming today."

"We're sorry, Jase." Deirdre spoke up. "We didn't want to spoil your day."

"*My* day? Today is my mom's day, not mine. But Steve should be here."

Jase walked into the throng in fellowship hall. He wondered why Steve chose Austin Justin Harry Harrison over his best friend. He wondered if he still had a best friend.

Odd how quickly a guy's mood can change. He shifted from confident everything would be okay to anger at being alone. No longer grateful, he slipped outside and blinked the burning from his eyes.

He didn't ask for this day. Or for a back-stabbing best friend.

He couldn't help but imagine his dad, wearing dress blues, and grinning from ear to ear the day his parents married. And, even as he tried to stay in the moment, he fought a twinge of resentment over today's celebration.

Guilt can be overwhelming. Guilt that washes over a kid like a tsunami. All because, if he could have his choice, he would choose to have never met Mr. Tims. He would choose to see his parents holding hands. He would choose life for his dad.

And only then could he possibly use the word dreamy. Well, okay. No. He would never use the word dreamy.

CHAPTER THIRTY-ONE

"Let's go find a burger." Pop placed his arm around Jase.

"Sounds good to me. But you should know, no one in Crumberry makes a burger as great as Juju's."

"That goes without saying. If we hang around here much longer, they will put us to work." He nodded toward Juju, Aunt Christy, Grandma Lynny, and a few friends from church.

Just a little while earlier, everyone gathered outside the fellowship hall and cheered as Sully and Janice made their way to Sully's truck. They left for their trip to an island paradise for a few days.

Jase was glad. A few days with Pop and Juju. A few days without dealing with the new Mr. Tims. A few days to figure out what the deal was with Steve.

Jase watched all the busy bees cleaning up the wedding fun. Pop was right, they'd better make a run for it.

Moments later, Jase shoved a fry in his mouth and slurped his strawberry shake.

"I'll let you know how this burger stacks up." Pop winked.

Joe's Burger Shack, nestled in the heart of downtown Crumberry, boasted the oldest eating establishment in the county. The iconic black- and white-checkered tile floors, speckled counter tops, and red leather stools screamed the 1950s. Booths lined the walls, and tables with red metal chairs dotted the dining room. Joe's claim to fame was his unlimited flavors of milkshakes. Jase tried many but always went back to his favorite, strawberry.

They took bites of their burgers and reached for extra napkins to wipe the mustard and mayo off their chins.

"Messy. But good." Pop took another bite.

They ate in silence. Not the awkward what-can-we-talk-about kind of silence. No. More like the we-don't always-have-to-be talking kind.

Jase wasn't about to waste a drop of strawberry shake goodness but the sound emanating from the straw shouted, "there's no more." Saddest. Sound. Ever.

"So, how's it going?" Pop slid the plastic basket of fries to the side.

"It. Well, what exactly is *it*?"

"Okay, if you want to play hardball. School. News of your teacher stepdad."

"At first, everyone stared and whispered. I thought maybe aliens took over my school during the Christmas break. Didn't last though. Either they stopped staring by the end of the week, or I stopped noticing."

"Maybe a little of both."

"I don't want to complain, but I'm more worried about Sully than I am the kids at school."

"Why?"

"He's just different. Like, last week I'm pretty sure he watched me with a microscope or magnifying glass. And he sent me to the principal's office without even hearing my side."

"Maybe he was stressed about the wedding, and he will be back to his old self once everything settles down. Try to be patient. Walk the line for a bit."

"Funny. That's exactly what he told me to do. Walk the line."

More silence followed as Jase thought about Pop's advice.

He wondered if Pop understood what he was trying to say. He wondered how long everything takes to settles down. He wondered why kids always have to walk the line when grown-ups make decisions kids don't like.

And he wondered why a large milkshake is never quite large enough.

She looked out the window at the ground below, growing ever smaller with each passing second.

"I can't believe we are actually married. And I can't believe we are getting away for a few days." Janice's heart flip-flopped inside her chest. "I haven't been away from Jase since ... well ... in a long time."

"He will be fine. I think he's excited to spend time with Pop and Juju. Maybe he will have a chance to talk with Pop. I'm sure Pop will help him work a few things out." Sully reached for her hand.

"What things?"

"Oh, nothing to worry about. Just had an issue at school this week. I handled it."

"How come I didn't know about this? What issues? Why didn't you tell me?"

"Jase and I decided not to add stress to your week. Really, Janice, everything is fine."

Her gaze returned to the window, now an amazing scene of bright blue sky and fluffy white clouds.

"Sully? Meeting your parents. Such a surprise. I wish you had told me first."

"I did tell you. I told everyone, remember?"

"I think it's odd you didn't tell me first. Odd, we've never even talked about them before and then ... surprise. They're here. What's their story? Tell me about them."

"I'm sorry I didn't tell you first. I didn't think ... well, I didn't think. And their story? It's quite a story. Can the story wait for another day?"

"I suppose. But no more surprises. Okay?"

"Deal."

The bright blue sky chased away her questions concerning Don and Margo Tims. Jase though. Nothing could remove Jase from her thoughts. She decided she would not spoil the trip with more questions and objections. The conversation could wait until they got home. Perhaps she should have had a talk with Sully long ago. A talk that made sure he understood there are no secrets in the Freeman-soon-to-be-Tims house.

But she watched the clouds float by and wondered why Jase didn't come to her. And how would she be able to convince him to talk to her. No. Matter. What.

CHAPTER THIRTY-TWO

Steve tossed the football into the air and caught it. He remembered what it felt like to be on the field. To hear the Crumberry Middle School fans call his name. To make his dad proud. He hated his concussion knocked him off the team. Or more accurately, his parents, doctor, and Coach K ganged up on him and ruled without his vote.

But one thing is sure—he is *not* a dumb jock. Jase knew his GPA never dipped below a 3.0. Why would Jase say something so mean? And untrue. Jealous much?

Skipping out on the wedding felt right. Inviting Harrison over for the day and making sure Haley knew it—well, that was genius.

Dumb jock, huh?

"You're really good at video games. I haven't played much since we moved. My game station isn't even unpacked yet." Harrison examined the controller as if seeing one for the first time. "I'm glad you're good at gaming. Jase warned me to let you win if I thought I might beat you. He said you're a real sore loser."

Steve's eyes burned at Harrison's comment.

"I guess I shouldn't have told you what he said, huh?" Harrison set the controller on the couch.

"Aw, don't worry 'bout it. Who cares what he has to say? Tell you what, I'll take it easy on you next time around. I didn't know you don't play much. I guess I just assumed ..." Steve shrugged.

"No worries. People assume a lot about me. I'm getting used to it."

Steve didn't know what to say. So he didn't say anything. But he decided to pay attention to the new kid.

And he decided he would wait for Jase's apology. Why should he go to Jase? Jase was the one who ran his mouth to Harrison.

Back at his desk, Jase thought through the events of the day. When he woke up this morning, life was still Team Freeman, and he had hopes of patching up his friendship with Steve. A mere twelve hours later, Team Tims drafted his mom and friendship with Steve moved to the almost-out-of-reach zone.

"Lecty, I wish I had the life of a bird. What do you have to worry about? Nothing. I make sure you have everything you need. I wonder where I would fly if I could grow wings. Somewhere trouble free. And you, Chesty. All you do all day is eat, sleep, and play. I wish I could be a dog for a day."

He closed his eyes and imagined a carefree day of eating, sleeping, and playing. Or maybe an afternoon of flying high above the troubles of life.

"Ahem. I said, AHEM!"

"Wha? What?" Jase shook his head and rubbed his eyes.

"You've lost sight of how great your life is."

"You can talk? You can talk!"

"Of course, I can talk. Can you hear? Are you listening?"

"I'm listening, I'm listening."

Chesty jumped up on Jase's bed and tilted his head to one side.

"I caaaaan taaaalk tooooooo!"

Jase jerked his head around and looked at Lecty. He hit the side of his head as if to knock the hallucinations out.

“I am not seeing and hearing what I think I am seeing and hearing. Am I?”

“Listen up. We have something to say.” Chesty’s ears wiggled as he spoke. “We think you are spoiled.”

“That’s riiiiiight. Spoiled.”

“We think you aren’t even trying to be thankful.”

“That’s riiiiight. Not even.”

“What would either of you know about life? I feed you. I make sure you have a place to sleep. I keep you safe. You don’t even know what you’re yapping about.”

“Think about it. Exactly.” Chesty laid down.

“That’s riiiiight.”

“We never leave 624 Juniper Street. We don’t get to go to school, hang out with friends, or know what it’s like to make choices. We’ll never have homework or go to a movie. We can’t even play video games.”

“And your point is?” Jase’s question hung in the air.

“You’re not tryyyyyyyying.” Lecty scolded.

“If you were listening, I wouldn’t have to explain this to you. All the stuff you complain about is the stuff life is made of. Choices, arguments, misunderstandings, forgiveness, and laughter. You whine about homework, friends, and a stepdad. Well, guess what?”

“I think you’re going to tell me.”

“Telllllll him. You better telllll him.” Lecty’s voice carried a mocking tone.

“Quit your bellyaching. Make the most of life. You’ve been given much, and much will be asked of you. Man up!”

A loud rap on the door caught Jase off guard, and he jumped. He rubbed his eyes and looked around. Chesty was curled up at the foot of his bed, snoring. Lecty stood on her perch, puffed up and beak tucked under her wing.

“Jase? Are you okay?” Juju knocked again.

"I ... I ... think so. Come in."

She opened the door. "Do you want a snack before bed? I can throw something together for you."

"No thanks, Juju, I'm not hungry. I won't be up much longer. I was going to try to read a little. I have to have this book read by Monday morning."

"Okay. Well, don't stay up too late. You can always read tomorrow. Goodnight. I'll see you in the morning."

He looked at his pets one more time. Whether they would say those things or not if they could speak, Jase got the message.

He knew many decisions were not his to make. But he had choices. He had power over his own perspective.

He could spend the rest of the weekend stewing, or he could get started reading. The Monday morning meeting with Austin Justin Harry Harrison and Madame President Madeline would be here soon—ready or not. He pulled the book from his backpack.

But there was something he needed to do first.

He bowed his head and prayed. He thanked God for his health and his home, for Pop and Juju, for choices. And for Team Tims.

CHAPTER THIRTY-THREE

"You're not wearing that to church, are you?" Pop met Jase in the hall.

Jase smoothed the front of his wrinkled T-shirt. "I didn't think we would be going to church today."

"Hmm, last I checked, today is Sunday."

"Gotcha." Jase retreated. Several minutes later, he entered the kitchen showered and in wrinkle-free, clean clothes.

"Don't you look sharp." Juju set a plate of pancakes in front of him. "Careful not to drip syrup on yourself." She winked at him.

"You clean up nice," Pop smirked.

"Tell me about the book you're reading. Did you finish last night?" Juju sipped her coffee.

"I'm reading *The Book Thief* for a project in literature. The story takes place during World War Two. I'm almost halfway through."

"Oh, that does sound interesting. You will have plenty of time to finish this afternoon. Well, plenty of time if this old man," she nodded at Pop, "will leave you alone long enough."

"Hey, now, don't blame me if the boy would rather spend time hearing stories from my youth instead of keeping his nose in a book."

"You need to learn how to hush every now and then." Her eyes twinkled at him. He reached over and patted her hand.

"I'd hoped to get to meet your best friend at the wedding. What's his name? Stuart? Sabastian? Sean?"

Jase chuckled. "Steve, Pop. He didn't come."

"Oh?"

"Yeah. Haley said he stayed home and invited the new kid from school over to play video games." Jase shoved a remaining bite of pancake around his plate. "May I be excused?"

"Sure. We'll leave in about twenty minutes." Juju sent a concerned glance across the table to Pop.

"Today's text comes from the book of Daniel. Please turn to Daniel chapter 1."

Maybe staying up late to read wasn't such a great idea.

Heavy eyelids.

Shoulders drooping.

Head bobbing.

Until.

He heard.

Pastor Jim say.

"Most scholars believe Daniel was around fourteen years old when he and his friends were taken into captivity."

What? Wow. Fourteen.

"Daniel had courage because he trusted the Lord to take care of him, even when his life was in danger. Daniel didn't try to handle life decisions on his own. He went to the Lord in prayer. He knew God would be with him, even if King Nebuchadnezzar threatened to harm him. We will see later, Daniel gave God the glory and credit for answering his prayers. The king had his own gods, Daniel needed courage to tell the king about the One True God."

Jase listened to Pop and Juju talk about the sermon and what a great job Pastor Jim did. Dixie's Café hummed around him, dishes clinking and clanking, people talking, and the occasional "order up" being called out.

"What can I get you folks?" The waitress pulled an ink pen from behind her ear and stood poised to write their orders down.

"I'll have a half club sandwich and your soup of the day, please." Juju closed her menu.

"Ham and cheese sub with BBQ chips, please." Jase's stomach growled.

"How's the roast beef today? Any good?" Pop couldn't just order without a conversation.

"Our roast beef is always good." She tapped the end of her pen on her notepad.

"I'll take a hot roast beef on rye with a side of sweet potato fries."

"Comin' right up."

"Old man, I think you might have insulted her with your questions."

"Aw, don't you worry. She knew I was just messing with her. Jase, you're awfully quiet over there. You okay?"

"Yeah ... I mean, yes, sir. Just thinking about what Pastor Jim said. Daniel wasn't much older than I am."

"Hard to imagine how he must have felt, being taken away from his family."

"He trusted God to help him man up. Chesty said I need to man up."

"Chesty said? Son, are you feeling okay?" Pop put his hand on Jase's forehead. "Hmm, no fever."

Jase coughed. "Did I say Chesty? I meant Pastor Jim. Yeah, Pastor Jim."

"Hey, Jase. What's up?" Andrew stepped up to their booth.

"Introduce us to your friend."

"This is Andrew."

Pop reached out his hand, "Hello, Andrew. We are Pop and Juju. Sit down and join us?"

Andrew rocked his weight from one foot to another.

"Yeah, you hungry? Eat with us."

"Uh. Thanks." Andrew slid in next to Jase.

Pop waved at their server and asked for another ham and cheese sub for their guest.

"I'm guessing you go to school together?"

"Andrew is in eighth grade, but we see each other around." Jase answered Juju and glanced at Andrew.

"Yeah, we see each other at lunch mostly."

Their food arrived, saving the day for Jase. He really didn't want to talk about the Table of Shame today. Instead, they chatted about stuff that didn't matter like the weather and the construction on the edge of town.

Andrew ate quietly. When the meal was finished, he stood and thanked Pop and Juju. He turned to Jase.

"I see and hear things. Just want you to know I'll help you. You're not what he says you are."

Andrew walked away.

Jase shrugged at Pop and Juju. He truly didn't know what Andrew meant. He wondered who said what. He wondered how Andrew planned to help him.

And he wondered, would God help him make the right choices Monday when he would meet with Austin Justin Harry Harrison? Would God show him how to fix his friendship with Steve?

And could God take his new, mixed team family, and somehow make everything okay?

CHAPTER THIRTY-FOUR

He spent the rest of the afternoon reading *The Book Thief*. He decided not to tell Pop he actually preferred reading over listening to stories. At least today, he preferred reading. A great book can take a kid, pick him up from his reality, and drop him in the middle of someone else's world.

He completed the reading and knew he could handle tomorrow morning's meeting with Harry and Madeline. Of course, all he really had to do was wait to be told what to do.

Jase and Chesty emerged from his room. Jase grabbed a jacket and the dog leash.

"I'm going to take Chesty for a walk. I won't be gone long."

"Bundle up. You'll freeze your knees out there." Juju called from the kitchen.

Pop reclined in Jase's favorite chair, hands folded over a newspaper opened across his chest. Snoring.

"Let's go, boy."

January in Crumberry is not the best month to have to walk a dog. Jase looked forward to spring. The temperature today registered a crisp twenty-nine degrees.

"Don't get too excited, bud. This walk will not be a long one."

And so they walked.

And without planning the destination, Jase found himself at Pickle Tree Park. The park was empty, not a soul in sight. The swings swayed in the winter winds. The bare branches on trees looked like hands with too many fingers reaching toward the sky as if they could snatch whatever might fly by.

He sat on the cold metal bench and scooped Chesty to his lap.

"This used to be my favorite place. See the pond? Me and my dad used to fish there. And Mom says I used to love to go down the slide over there. I don't remember, but I'm sure it's true."

Even as he sat in the freezing air, he let his mind go back in time, and his mood was good. He expected sadness to creep in while remembering the big one that got away or the day he scared his mom when he fell in. He could almost feel his dad's strong hands as he recalled the rescue.

No. No sadness.

Just a warm contentment over good times.

Warmth that almost made him forget the twenty-nine degrees he and Chesty were walking in.

But not quite.

"Let's go, boy. I promise we'll come back on the first warm day. You're going to love it here. I promise."

He set the pudgy puppy on the frigid ground, and they began the trek back home. Chesty led the way. Cold air did not impress him.

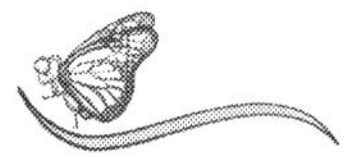

Jase and Chesty were almost home when a brown minivan arrived, pulling into the driveway of 624 Juniper Street.

He slowed his pace so he could get a glimpse of who occupied the old van.

The driver's side door opened.

The tall thin man with the whirly curly mustache stepped out. He walked around the front of the van to the passenger side and opened the door.

The lady with short brown hair that curled around her face emerged.

Don and Margo Tims.

Chesty barked and growled at the sight of a strange vehicle and people he didn't know.

"It's okay, boy. They aren't here for trouble."

"Hey, there! Who is your furry friend? I hope he knows we are friends too." Mr. Don Tims waved at Jase. Margo Tims placed her hand in the crook of Don Tims' elbow.

"His bark is worse than his bite. By a lot. 'Cause, well, he doesn't bite."

"We hope you don't mind we've stopped by." Jase watched her hair as she spoke. Nope. The hair did not move. Perhaps the hair wasn't hair at all. Wood, maybe?

Stop staring. Stop staring.

"Mom and Sully aren't here. Just Pop, Juju, and me."

"And your furry friend."

"Yes. Mr. and Mrs. Tims, meet Chesty."

"Call us Don and Margo. After all, we are family now." He twisted one end of his twirly mustache.

Jase led the way to Pop and Juju all the while wondering where Don and Margo came from and why Sully had never talked about them.

"Come in. Come in." Juju motioned for the Timses to sit on the couch. She walked over and patted Pop on the foot. "Wake up, old man. We have guests."

He grunted and stirred. Opened one eye and sat up straight. "Oh! Hello, hello. We met yesterday. Sure did, yes, we met yesterday." Pop ran his hand through his hair and rubbed his eyes.

"We're sorry to disturb you. But we wanted to come by and say hello to the boy before we leave." He did it again. Twisted the end of the 'stache.

"He was about to wake up anyway." Juju shot a frown at Pop. "May I get you something to drink? Some tea, maybe?"

"No, thank you. We won't keep you long." He turned to Jase. "As we told you yesterday, Sullivan has told us a lot about you. Unfortunately, we haven't had much time to spend with him in recent years."

"Our work doesn't allow us to contact family when we are out of the country." Margo spoke with a whisper.

"Seriously? What do you do? Where have you been? Were you gone a long time?" Jase hadn't intended for the questions to come flying out of his mouth at warp speed. "Oh ... uh ... I'm sorry. I didn't mean to be rude."

"We're glad you're curious. Unfortunately, we cannot answer your questions. Our work is, well, quite sensitive. However, we brought you a gift."

Don Tims, the man with the whirly twirly mustache, reached into his jacket pocket and retrieved a small wooden box.

CHAPTER THIRTY-FIVE

Jase peered into the small box.

"Lapis Lazuli." Don Tims sat with perfect posture.

"The timeless deep blue gemstone." Margo's voice smiled.

Jase rolled the smooth, round gemstone in between his finger and thumb.

"Why, I don't think I've ever seen anything quite so blue!" Juju looked on in amazement.

"Some people say Lapis Lazuli is the most beautiful gemstone in the world. We brought the gem back from where we work. If you read up on gems, you'll learn Lapis is a universal symbol for wisdom and truth. We couldn't think of a more perfect gift for you as your family begins a new chapter." Don explained with precision.

"The stone reminds me of a marble, but a marble is heavier. You're right, Juju, the blue is the bluest blue ever." Jase held the gemstone up in the light, examining the treasure closely.

"This stone is described as timeless blue. When you look at it, we want you to be reminded God is truly timeless. He never changes. In fact, an important part of his message to us is he will always be who he has always been. You can count on God." Margo's eyes sparkled as she spoke.

"Thank you. I'll take good care of it, I promise."

"Oh, but we want you to take greater care of your relationship with the One who created the gemstone. The gem is simply a pretty rock. A rock without power. The One who will always be who he has always been is the source of all power. At the end of the day, this is simply a beautiful rock that can be damaged or lost. But your relationship with God ... well, God cannot be destroyed. Do you know how great his love is for you, Jase?" Don spoke of God's love with ease.

"I'm not sure I'll ever really understand, Mr. Don. But I do know God loves me." Jase continued to roll the gemstone.

"You've added a stepdad to your family, and we know that means changes that aren't always easy. Remember while you are adjusting, God is always busy, working for your good and his glory." Like Don, Margo's words flowed comfortably.

Pop sat, watched, and listened. Jase peeked over at him and wondered why he was being so quiet. Pop was not a quiet man.

"Well, we must be going. We have a plane to catch and much to do before returning to our assignment." Don stood and held his hand out to his wife to help her to her feet.

"Assignment? Where are you going? What is your job?" Jase genuinely wanted to know the details of this mysterious and odd couple's life.

"Our story is not to be told today. We will save it for another day." He turned to Juju. "We thank you for welcoming us. As we pray for Sullivan, we will also pray for you all. We trust God to take care of you until we meet again."

"Jase, may I hug you?" Had there ever been a more gentle voice in all the world?

"Yes, ma'am." Jase hugged the short woman with the hair that curled around her face. He shook the hand of the tall man with the whirly twirly mustache.

Margo placed her hand in the crook of Don's elbow. Jase watched Don open the door for Margo.

He gripped the timeless blue gemstone in the palm of his hand. He could close his eyes and see the brilliant blueness. And deep in his heart, he purposed to take greater care of his relationship with the One who created the treasure and would always be who he has always been.

He wondered about these peculiar people. Before yesterday, he didn't know whether they existed or not. They appeared today and sat in his living room. Bearing gifts. They spoke of God's love as easily as one would talk about a lifelong friend. And for some strange reason, he felt like he had known them always.

"Lapis Lazuli. Timeless blue gemstone." He whispered the words as he typed into the search engine.

The history of the ancient stone fascinated him.

He kept reading until he located the places this Lapis Lazuli is mined.

Russia, the Andes Mountains in Chili, Myanmar, Tajikistan, and Pakistan. But the most highly regarded Lapis Lazuli is mined in ...

He blinked.

He swallowed hard.

And he said it out loud.

"Afghanistan."

CHAPTER THIRTY-SIX

He tossed all night, dreaming of blue stones, blue mustaches, blue cake, and blue algebra textbooks. He ran from rolling blue stones in Afghanistan and watched men in blue fatigues fire their weapons at blue pancakes.

As if narrating the dreams, he heard Juju saying "don't you look sharp," Pop told him many times to "roll with the punches," and Andrew repeated "I will help you."

He walked the blue halls of Crumberry Middle School, searching for Steve and hiding from Harrison. Sully, dressed in blue, stepped from behind every corner and peered through every blue-tinted window.

Bam!

Jase slammed into the floor. He rolled over and rubbed his forehead, pulling his hand away as the searing pain screamed at him.

"Oh, Jase. Oh, my. Are you okay? You're not okay. Don't sit up yet. Stay put. Pop! Bring a bag of vegetables from the freezer!" Juju's eyes widened and her face grew pale.

"I'm okay, Juju. Just a crazy dream. That's all."

"And a goose-egg on your forehead."

Pop arrived with a bag of peas, and Juju held it to his head.

"Maybe I'm not okay." He winced.

"Juju, you can breathe. The boy is fine. Let him sit up."

She helped him place his back against his bed as the color returned to her face.

"You ought not scare an old lady." She fanned herself with her hand.

"Must have been some kind of scary dream to get you to leap from your bed."

"Not scary. Just weird. Really weird."

"Well, you're going to have a real headache. Probably all day." Pop whistled.

"Maybe you should stay home."

"I'm okay, Juju. I can't miss today. I promise I'll call if I can't handle it."

"I have breakfast ready whenever you are. Move slowly, okay? Pop will drive you to school in time for your library meeting. Only if you're sure you're okay." Juju wrung her hands.

They helped him up to the edge of his bed, made sure he wasn't dizzy, and left his room so he could get dressed.

He touched the bump on his head once again.

Ay-yi-yi that hurts. Bet it's going to bruise. Probably a big blue bruise. Now that's almost funny.

Jase opened the door to the library. He was surprised to see his team weren't the only ones meeting this morning.

Madeline snapped her fingers, and Jase obeyed like a well-trained dog.

"Hey, where's Harrison?"

"Not here yet. That means he gets the leftovers. You snooze ya lose." Madeline looked up from her book. "Whoa, what happened to you?"

"Just a bump on the head, that's all. Don't overreact."

She shrugged. But she continued to stare. He brushed his hair over the bump, but the attempt to hide the hideous injury was useless.

"I'm good at art, so I get dibs on an illustration."

"Fine with me," she said. "I'll take writing an alternate ending, and Harrison can ..."

"Can what?" He stepped up from behind Madeline. "What happened? That looks like it hurts worse than a ..."

"Don't say it."

"What? Why not? Finish, Harrison." Madeline placed her hands on her hips.

"Worse than a poke in the eye with a sharp stick."

She scrunched her nose and tossed her hair over her shoulder. No words. Just a half confused, half disgusted expression covered her face.

"Told ya not to say it."

"We've already decided. You get the memory work."

"What if I don't want to memorize anything?"

"You get what you get. Don't throw a fit." And she picked up her books and walked away.

"How does she do that?" Her total control of the assignment baffled him. "And stop looking at me."

"That ... that thing on your head is like a bad accident. I don't want to look but I can't look away."

Jase rolled his eyes and immediately wished he hadn't. *Ow*

"It's the bluest bump I've ever seen."

Harrison walked away.

Jase Freeman.

In the library.

With a blue goose egg.

CHAPTER THIRTY-SEVEN

"Haley, wait up. Did you see Jase yet today?"

"No, he wasn't on the bus this morning. I won't see him until lunch. Why?"

"Oh, um. Never mind."

She bit the corner of her lip and tapped her foot.

"Okay. He's mad at you. Not a little mad. Like, a lot mad."

"Harrison, don't exaggerate. Jase isn't angry with me. I didn't do anything."

"I'm just trying to warn you. You might want to give him time to cool down."

"Did he say anything? How do you know he's mad?"

"I don't know. Maybe the steam rolling outta his ears? I asked what was wrong, and he gritted his teeth, and I'm pretty sure maybe he said your name under his breath."

Haley's expression said it all. She had never been one to control her facial expressions. And at this moment, she didn't even try. The pieces of the trouble-making Harrison puzzle were beginning to fall into place, and she had no time for his games.

"What? Don't look at me like that." Harrison's voice quivered a bit.

This is new. Haven't seen Harrison nervous yet. Yeah, pretty sure he's a troublemaker. But why?

"You're pretty sure? Maybe? What's with you, Harrison? It's almost like you don't want friends."

She pushed her glasses up, gave him one more stern look, and left Harrison standing alone.

Everyone says girls are the ones who love drama. Right. Whatever.

"Get with your groups and be sure you are all on the same page of your project. Get it? On the same *page*?" Miss Teal's attempt at a joke was met by blank faces. "Well, okay then. After you've met, you will find supplies on the back table for those of you who are illustrating a scene. Those of you writing and memorizing don't need supplies and can get busy at your desk. I'll give you fifteen minutes to meet. Get busy."

Chairs scooting and beehive-like low, rumbly voices.

The boys sat in front of Madeline's desk like obedient toddlers.

And waited.

"Harrison, let us know what passage you are going to memorize. Jase, have you decided what you will illustrate?"

"I'm going to illustrate Liesel standing outside her foster home with Hans and Rosa Hubbermann."

"Okay. Good, good. Harrison?" Madeline clicked her fingernails on her desk.

"I don't know yet. Any suggestions?"

"Make up your own mind, Harrison. Choose something easy, if you're not up to a challenge." Jase didn't mean to sound snarky. But yeah. He sounded snarky.

He looked over the supplies and chose a sharp pencil and a poster board.

He had already thought it through. A distraught Liesel, standing alone in front of her foster home doesn't need color. Nazi Germany. World War II.

He pulled some scratch paper from his backpack and sketched a few German World War II-era houses like the ones he'd searched the internet to find. If his houses could speak, they would tell stories of horrors and destruction. Of hate and loneliness. Of what happens when people forget there's a God who doesn't hate people.

And as he scribbled out the war-torn structures, he remembered what his Pop told him over Christmas break when he asked why God allows bad things to happen. Pop said, "There are no puppets in the world, Jase. Only people who make choices. Choices for good or for evil. Don't you forget, even when people choose evil, God is working. He doesn't overlook evil. All you can do is trust him and choose to obey what he says to do."

I guess being snarky wasn't the best choice.

CHAPTER THIRTY-EIGHT

"Hey." Jase sat next to Danny. "Where's Harrison?"

Haley shrugged.

Deirdre didn't look up from her lunch tray.

Steve looked away and acted as if he didn't hear the question.

The cafeteria hummed from conversations taking place at every table except the one where Jase sat.

The table that used to hold friendship and stories and laughter.

The table that once held forgiveness and understanding even when they couldn't possibly understand.

"What's wrong with everyone? Steve? Are you ever going to speak to me again? Haley?"

She glanced at him and looked away. "What, decided you're no longer mad at me?"

"Mad at ... what are you talking about?"

Awkward. Silence.

Jase shoved his tray to the center of the table and stood. He waited a second or two for someone to say something. *Anything.*

He left his chicken nuggets and baked beans and started for the exit.

"Hey, finished already?" Harrison grinned as he spoke.

Jase paused and tried to think of a response. *No, only snark here.* He exited the cafeteria.

"I guess Jase is too good to eat with us." Harrison began eating as soon as he sat down. "Just as well," he said in between bites. "He's not as good a friend as you guys think. He just said 'who needs them?' before he left."

Steve turned his head and inspected Harrison.

Haley's shoulders dropped.

Deirdre's eyes remained downcast.

Danny quietly ate.

"I tried to stop him, but he wouldn't listen. Hey, is anyone going to eat his chicken nuggets?"

What Harrison didn't see and no one else noticed ... was Andrew. Seated at his table. Just within earshot of both the short exchange between Harrison and Jase, and the remarks the new kid made at the table of friends.

No one knew he listened.

No one could see the wheels turning in his mind, his thoughts as he finished the last bites of broccoli on his tray.

And most certainly, no one was aware of the friendship that formed at the Table of Shame.

Or Andrew's resolve to somehow stop this new kid from wrecking CMS for Jase Freeman.

CHAPTER THIRTY-NINE

At first, he jogged. Moments later he ran. Heart pounding, sweat pouring, as if his-life-was-at-stake kind of running. The tears pushed from behind his eyes, threatening to spill over like the waters of Niagara Falls.

He didn't care.

Instead of caring, he ran.

Harder.

Pushing.

Until his lungs burned and his legs screamed for rest.

Perhaps, if he ran long enough and hard enough, he could outrun every worry and misunderstanding sitting between his shoulder blades, relentlessly poking and prodding.

His mom would say, "Stop being so dramatic."

"Go with the flow and roll with the punches." Pop's advice handed down through the generations.

He could almost hear Haley, "Why are boys so stupid?"

Mrs. Zimmers told him to "hold your head high and keep your sense of humor."

And Steve ...

Well, Steve ... would he say anything to him ever again?

"Freeman. FREEMAN!"

Spaghetti legs unable to hold him any longer, he crumpled to the floor in a sweaty, sprawled mess. Each beat of his heart pounded a reminder of all his worries, the pulse of stress running through the goose egg on his forehead.

"Here." Couch K handed him a bottle of water. "What's going on with you?"

He sat up and leaned against the basketball players' bench. Sweat dripped, coming together to form little rivers of fire that streamed right over his goose egg. He grimaced as he gingerly patted his forehead.

"Just sit here until you catch your breath."

Thankful.

Grateful.

Relieved.

When he stepped into the gym and began his run, he had not intended to bust his guts. He ran without thought. What would he have done had there been anybody in the gym? How much worse could his life have been if some busybody bunch of girls or muscle-flexing too big for their own good group of guys saw the spectacle?

The cool water soothed his parched throat.

"Okay, you need to walk it off. Can you walk?" Coach K helped him to his feet.

Coach walked alongside Jase, making one lap around the gym, the only sound between them the squeak of their gym shoes on the shiny gym floor.

"I used to do the same thing when I was your age. Sometimes, I'd get so angry or whatever, I didn't know what to do with myself. Felt like I might crawl out of my own skin. So I'd run. I'd run until I could run no more. All my energy going into being afraid or frustrated poured right out of me into the running. I'm pretty sure running kept me out of trouble."

"Hard to imagine you ever being afraid." Jase took another drink of water.

"Everybody gets afraid sooner or later. You want to talk about it?"

"No, I don't think so."

"The gym is always open and almost always empty during lunch. My door is always open too. And listen up. No matter what you are going through today or this week or even this school year—I promise life will ease up and get better. This too shall pass."

"Thanks, Coach. Life sure can stink sometimes."

Coach rubbed his nose and rolled his eyes, whistled, and said, "Life's not the only thing that stinks right now. How about you wash up and grab a Crumberry Wildcats T-shirt from my office. You can pay me later."

Thankful.

Grateful.

Relieved.

He would clean up and finish this day without the psst, psst, psst, of a busybody bunch of girls or too big for their own good group of guys.

Surely the worst of this day was behind him. Head held high ...

CHAPTER FORTY

He stood in the hall.

Looking into the algebra room.

In disbelief.

Mrs. Ruppert. The meanest substitute teacher at Crumberry Middle School.

His thoughts went into gameshow mode, even playing upbeat trumpety kind of background music while the voice in his head introduced the next contestant ...

"Let's give a big welcome to Mrs. Ruppert, coming to us from the stuffy algebra classroom at Crumberry Middle School. Mrs. Ruppert enjoys bringing nausea to the students with her wild animal print clothes and ca-ray-zey colors. She's even painted her creepy long nails a glow-in-the-dark orange. Her hobbies are causing middle school kids to sweat with her narrow-eyed glare she's perfected over time and showing Jase Freeman yes, yes, Jase ... your day can always get worse."

I'm gonna hold my head high but ... sense of humor? Not today.

He slipped into his seat and opened his textbook. No way was he going to get into trouble today.

No.

Way.

She closed the door as the tardy bell sounded. She turned to face the class and the door opened, bumping her from behind and nearly knocking her off balance. Muffled giggles and snorts popped up across the room.

Austin Justin Harry Harrison slipped in and attempted to walk to his seat.

"Freeze!" Her narrow-eyed glare stifled the laughs. "You're late!"

"Technically, I made it in before the bell quit ringing."

Gasp! Did poor Harry really just correct Mrs. Ruppert? Looks like today is Harry's day.

"Name!"

"Harrison Peterson, ma'am." He turned to face her. "I'm sorry. I'm new here. I'm still learning the halls and the classrooms, and I haven't made any friends yet so there's no one here to help me find my way. It won't happen again, ma'am. I promise."

She sucked her teeth for a moment, as if she were trying to get the last bit of lunch out from in between them. Kids leaned forward in their desks in anticipation of the punishment to come. The squirrels, often a distraction during boring algebra moments, stopped chasing each other in the trees.

The music played in Jase's head. The wah-wah-wah he hears right before the words "game over" float on the screen.

"Very well. Be seated. See to it you keep your word."

Huh?

Wha ...?

Austin Justin Harry Harrison turned to walk to his seat. He paused and looked right at Jase. And he smiled. And nodded his head. It wasn't a hey, how ya doin kind of smile. No. It was a that's how you do it kind of smile.

Had he really just witnessed the new kid get away with coming in late *and* being a little snarky with Mrs. Ruppert? Did he really just hear her give him another chance?

And did he really just say he has no friends at Crumberry Middle School?

CHAPTER FORTY-ONE

"Mr. Tims left instructions for you to complete the remaining sections of chapter forty-three. I require you to accomplish this task in silence. If you have a question, raise your hand and wait for me to recognize you. Mind your business, use your time wisely, and you'll have no homework. But if you play, you'll pay."

And with that she sat behind Mr. Tims's desk, pulled a magazine out of her massive leopard print bag and began flipping pages. Jase figured she was just looking at the pictures. He wondered what else was in her bag. A flat screen television or maybe a ham? Could be both.

She cleared her throat, and his stare snapped from her bag to her face. Her expressionless, motionless, stone-cold face. Eyes wide with fear, he focused on chapter forty-three and didn't look up until he heard freedom ring.

Kids clamored ahead of him, apparently more eager than he to escape algebra and Mrs. Ruppert.

"Jase Freeman."

He stopped in his tracks. "Ma'am?"

"I'm not sure what you found so interesting at the beginning of class. I suggest from here forward you keep your mind on algebra and don't concern yourself with anything else."

"Yes, ma'am."

"And take care of that hideous knot on your head."

"Yes, ma'am."

Was there a hint of caring in her voice? Couldn't be. This goose-egg is messing with my hearing.

Andrew stood in a corner and watched kids pour into the hall, crossing paths, briefly talking, hurrying on their way to the final class of the day.

He didn't speak to anyone. He watched Harrison Peterson exit algebra. Seconds later, he saw Jase turn toward the gym. Steve came through along with Haley.

"Yeah, well I'm not happy about it either. Don't ask me how it happened or how to fix. Not my problem, ya know?" He held both hands in the air.

"Steve, you have to care—our friendships are falling apart." Haley's voice cracked.

"I do care. Seems I care more than Jase does. What do you want me to do?" Steve raised the volume with each word.

Haley dropped her head.

Jase finished gym class without getting himself into trouble. He did exactly what Coach K said to do and was super thankful Coach K didn't mention what they both knew. The pressure inside Jase was building. And he was running out of ways to handle the stress.

How far and how hard can a guy run? And does all the heart-bursting, oxygen-depriving one foot in front of the other therapy lift the weight of life or just make it hard to breathe for a while?

CHAPTER FORTY-TWO

The last bus pulled away from Crumberry Middle School. The squeak of tennis shoes in the gym told Harrison the basketball team was practicing.

He meandered to the door and peered in. Yes, half of the gym was consumed by CMS's tallest. On the other half, the CMS cheer squad gathered to rehearse their skills.

Harrison slipped in and climbed to the top bleacher.

Look at them. All of them. Team players, or at least they look like a team. I bet they really hate each other or are jealous when one hits a three pointer. Same for the cheerleaders. Everybody likes to pretend they are friends.

Harrison watched, unseen by either team. His mind wandered while he looked on. He thought about each move his family had made in the past four years. Too many to count. He would have recalled the names of the guys he considered friends, but hard as he tried, none came to mind. That's what happens when you're always the new kid.

"Hey, you're the new kid, right?" Coach K motioned to Harrison to come to him.

He wanted to roll his eyes or make a smart mouthed response. Maybe he would have if he weren't intimidated by Coach K.

"Yes, sir." He shifted his weight from one foot to the other. "But, Coach, how long do I have to be here before I'm no longer the new kid?"

"Good question. I guess until the next new kid arrives."

"How often does a new family with kids move to Crumberry?"

"Hmm. Well. I'm sorry, son, but you're the first in a few years."

His eyes fell to his sneakers.

"Maybe you'll stop being the new kid as soon as you find your place." Coach K nodded toward the guys running drills. "Do you know much about basketball?"

"Some."

"Some?"

"Enough."

"Enough to keep the books?"

Harrison raised one eyebrow and looked up at Coach.

"Well? Want the job or not?"

"I know enough. I want the job."

"Great! Come to my office and I'll get you started. You need a wildcat jersey to wear to the games. I'll give you a schedule and we'll go over how it's done."

Harrison followed closely behind Coach K, watching the team as he walked.

Is the bookkeeper part of the team?

The CMS boys' basketball players knew the drills and worked together as if they could read each other's minds. Passing and shooting with precision, the team expected a great season ahead.

"Thank you, Mr. Peterson. Basketball is a fast game. You'll need to be on your toes to keep up." They walked out of the office and Coach motioned toward the court.

"I can do it, Coach." And Harrison left the gym.

A very tall, eighth-grade young man stepped off the court and wiped the sweat from his eyes. He reached for a bottle of water and guzzled it.

He watched Harrison Peterson walk and talk with Coach. He saw the scorebook tucked under the new kid's arm.

Andrew smiled.

CHAPTER FORTY-THREE

"I was thinking, you and Juju should take me back to Kentucky with you. I could finish school online. I could work on the farm."

"As much as we would love to have you, you know that would never work."

"Can't you at least talk with Juju? And my mom, you'd have to convince her."

"Juju would not object to having you. Your mom isn't the problem either."

"Then why? Why can't I finish the school year with you?"

"Because, running away is never the answer."

Jase slid from the couch to the floor, and Chesty climbed into his lap.

"You're almost a man, and you need to learn a man's way of handling the stuff no one likes to handle. A real man doesn't run, and he doesn't try to fix misunderstandings on his own. A real man turns to God and trusts him to work it all out. Trusts everything will be okay."

"That's easy to say. I'm not sure I know how to trust God. I trust you because I can see you and talk with you. I know you. But I can't see God. And he doesn't answer me like you do."

Pop reached down and scratched Chesty behind the ears. "How did you get to know me?"

"Huh? I mean, sir?"

"How did you get to know me well enough to trust me? I mean, just a few months ago I wasn't much more than a name and a few memories from your past."

"I spent time with you in December. We worked side by side on the treehouse. You told me stories, and you taught me a bunch of stuff."

"God doesn't talk out loud but he still talks. You get to know him the same way you got to know me. Spend time with him. He has a way of speaking to you without words. Do you trust me?"

"I think I trust you more than anyone else."

"Then you know I would never lie to you. Spend time with God. Read the Bible Juju gave you. Listen with your heart."

"I'll try, Pop. I want to know him. But I still want to run away to the farm."

"You remember the farm like you didn't have any cares there, but you did. Life is full of hassle. But when you respond right, hassles and stress will push you closer to God. Listen with your heart."

He stood at his bedroom window and looked at the stars. How many times had he looked out at the night sky and imagined what it would be like to fly or maybe swing from star to star?

They reminded him of God's realness and hugeness. He knew, when he looked at the expanse, God is large and in charge. Knowing God created great stuff gave him a sense of security. If God cared enough to know the stars by name, surely he cared for a kid who would rather run away than face the unknown. And he figured he could somehow learn to listen with his heart.

Gazing at the night lights used to be a family thing. Just the three of them. Then the two of them.

A shiver ran down as his spine.
And now there is one.

CHAPTER FORTY-FOUR

The bus pulled up just as Jase arrived. Perfect timing to skip awkward non-conversation.

He watched the houses roll by and tried not to think. Because thinking set his neck ablaze. Thinking tied his stomach in knots and made him want to scream.

How can Steve let the new guy cause trouble like this? I thought he knew me. He does know me! And what's with Haley? Sully. Mr. Tims. Mr. You-Better-Tow-The-Line Tims. I think maybe CMS has dropped into the Bermuda Triangle or the Twilight Zone. Or maybe down the rabbit hole in Alice in Wonderland. Everything is upside down.

Haley sat three seats in front of him. She usually sat next to him. Chattering like a chipmunk and jibber jabbering about her dog. He never in a million years thought he would miss it. All he could imagine while she talked is how nice some silence would be. But now that he had the quiet, well, he would rather hear about the new trick Snoodles learned or "how cute she is when she tilts her head and looks like she might say something."

Austin Justin Harry Harrison, where did you come from? I mean, do we really know anything about the guy? Maybe he's a Russian spy or an undercover operative from deep inside Afghanistan. Why was Haley so eager to invite him into our circle? Is she a plant?

He checked his smartwatch. Twenty more minutes until they would reach the school. He went back to watching the houses and streets pass by with hypnotizing sway.

"Get up. Are you just going to stay on the bus all day?"

He squinted a side-glance her way.

"What's it to you?"

"I was told to tell you Harrison would like to speak to you in the library. Documentary section. Don't be late." She spun on her heel, ponytail swishing as she marched off the bus. *Must be why it's called a ponytail. I suppose it keeps the flies away.*

He swung his backpack over one shoulder.

Music.

Strange music.

Coming from ... where?

Jase rubbed his eyes and looked again. His classmates blurred past him. No one spoke. The only sound was music. Madeline sauntered by, and he opened his mouth to speak but no words came out.

Harrison. In the library. Near the documentary volumes. He wore a black hat pulled down over his black, sunglass-covered eyes. The collar of his yellow polo shirt pulled straight up.

Bermuda Triangle. Twilight zone. A rabbit hole to Wonderland.

Harrison nodded his head. Jase followed.

"Don't speak. My people have informed me it's time. I must finish what I came here to accomplish. Don't get in my way."

Jase looked around. More students, stoically moving from one place to another like worker bees.

The music reached a crescendo. Drums and horns. Jase covered his ears and squished his eyes closed.

One Mississippi, two Mississippi, three Mississippi ...

Right eye opened, slightly. Hands off ears.

No music.

No Harrison.

I'm on the bus. I'm on the bus?

Eyes wide open, wild with confusion, Jase checked his surroundings. The bus slowed and the sounds of classmates on their way to class floated in when the doors swooped open.

Haley, still seated three rows ahead of him, stirred and gathered her things.

Was it yesterday's blue goose egg at work, causing visions and dreams and weird hallucinations?

Or maybe his brain had begun to pack in preparation of running away.

CHAPTER FORTY-FIVE

I'm late, I'm late, no time to say hello, goodbye. I'm late, I'm late, I'm late.

Jase barreled around the corner, the second bell blaring through the halls. His sneakers skidded to a stop just short of plowing into Harrison.

"Slow down, you could hurt someone, don't ya know."

"Yeah. Whatever. I'm late. You are too. Move it."

"Wow. Rude."

Jase blew into homeroom.

Mr. Houston raised both eyebrows but didn't say anything. Principal Drew droned on with announcements, and Jase took the time to catch his breath.

"Be sure to come on out and support the Wildcats basketball team this Friday as we take on the fighting Pirates. And remember, it's never a crummy day at Crumberry Middle School."

"Go make it a great Tuesday. Don't allow anyone to tell you it can't be done." Mr. Houston stood at the door, joking with students as they left his room.

"Goose egg is looking better, Jase. More light yellow and less blue."

"Progress."

He chuckled. "Hold on to your progress, son. No steps backward."

Jase gave Mr. Houston thumbs up and stepped into the hall to face the day.

As surviving the day was his number one goal, he pushed through science with no bumps in the road. He persevered and pushed towards literature. At least he could use the next hour or so to sketch his illustration for the group project. No one talking at him or to him. No demands or questions.

Sweet silence.

"Good morning, get right to work on your part of your group project. I'll let you know when we have about fifteen minutes remaining and you can get together to be sure you are all on the same page. We will begin presenting tomorrow."

How does she do it? Every day. Always smiling. Always patient.

He wasn't thrilled about those last minutes of class, but he decided he would survive. He wondered how Madeline got to be so good at taking charge without apology. Her approach to the group project made it possible to hear less from Harrison and get right to work.

"Well? Let's hear it. First few lines are all we need." Madeline made notes in her binder. "What are you waiting for? Do not tell me you don't have your part memorized yet. Do not even."

Harrison just stood there. Mouth hanging open like a cave.

Jase enjoyed the moment. A little too much, perhaps. He knew he shouldn't be happy at Harrison's expense. But watching Mr. Know-it-all squirm under Madam Madeline's gaze was pretty much the best minute of the week.

"Well?"

"Back off, ay? I'm working on it. I'll be fine with my part when our turn rolls around."

"You better be. I already told you boys I don't want my GPA suffering because of a stupid video game or whatever it is boys do when they should be working. Jase? Are you ready?"

Jase held his sketch up for his group to see.

Silence.

But was it a good kind of silence?

"Wow, Jase. I didn't know you were so good. It's really good. I mean, *really* good. I feel like I'm there. And those shades and lines. You make me feel the gloom. What an awful time in history."

"Thanks. I'm almost finished. I'll be ready."

"I'm almost finished, as well. I think we will earn a good grade. Well ... we *better* anyway." She turned her face to Harrison. "If you need help, I'm sure Jase would be glad to meet with you after school."

"Wait. I would?"

Madeline shot a look Jase's way. Her special powers of persuasion wrapped around him like a boa constrictor coiling its prey.

"Yeah, yeah. I would. Just let me know." He slunk back to his desk, wondering once again—*how does she do that?*

CHAPTER FORTY-SIX

He wasn't exactly sure why, but he decided to try lunch with the gang one more time. Surely today could be better than yesterday.

Too far away to hear what was being said, he scanned the table of friends as he approached. Steve, laughing, eating, and laughing again. Haley and Deirdre chatting, both were animated and they sometimes spoke at the same time but neither seemed to notice. Danny, watching, listening and nodding. Typical Danny.

And Harrison.

Sitting near Steve.

"I finally unpacked my game station last night. Want to come over some time?"

"Yeah. Let me know when you feel like losing bigtime."

"Yeah, okay."

"Is that all you talk about?" Haley rolled her eyes.

"Sometimes we talk about sports. Like basketball. Who is going to the game Friday night?" Steve raised his hand as he asked.

"Didn't I tell you? I'm keeping the books. I'll be there front and center."

"Good for you, little buddy!"

Jase stood at the table with precision timing. *Did Steve call Austin Justin Harry Harrison little buddy?* The mashed sweet potatoes and greasy green beans weren't very appetizing anymore. *Go with the flow and roll with the punches.*

He slid his tray by Danny. "Hey, what's up? Do these beans taste as bad as they look?"

Awkward silence.

Jase scooped a bite of potatoes and eyeballed his friends. "Well?"

"They aren't too bad." Danny mumbled.

"Anyway, what did you say? You're keeping the books? Way to go!"

"I think I was at the right place at the right time, that's all."

"Are you sure you can keep up? Keeping the books is an important job." Deirdre paused her conversation with Haley. "I don't think we will be at the game. Sorry. But I think sports are a waste of time."

Steve stopped chewing and stared. His face contorted, clearly confused by her statement.

"I wouldn't miss it." Haley, always positive and kind. "Harrison, I know you'll do a great job."

"The game Friday? I'll be there. Go, Wildcats!" Jase's insecurity broke through the cracks in his voice.

More. Awkward. Silence.

Danny kept his face toward his lunch tray. Deirdre bit the corner of her lip and looked at Haley who looked at Steve.

Steve looked at Harrison and took another bite. He stood and grabbed his tray.

"Hey, we have time before third period, let's go hang out in the gym. See who else is there."

"Don't bother. I'll leave."

Jase didn't wait to find out if anyone would object and ask him to stay. He left his tray and walked out.

Haley wiped a tear that escaped as soon as Jase left.

"This isn't right. We need to fix it. Steve, he's your best friend."

"Honestly, I'm not sure why you are trying so hard, Haley. I don't think you know him like you think you do." Harrison smirked.

"Do you ever *really* know a person?" Deirdre asked.

"Seems to me the one we don't know is *you*, Harrison." Danny finally had something to say.

All the air left the cafeteria, and the stunned friends looked on in amazement at Danny's sudden bravery.

Deirdre swallowed hard.

Haley's eyes widened, and Steve showed no emotion.

Harrison's right eye twitched. He took a deep breath and exhaled as if he had the rest of the day.

"No need to be cruel, Danny. Everyone knows I'm new here. I haven't done anything but speak up and tell you what I thought you would want to know."

The once solid group of friends, one by one, set their gaze on Steve.

Steve set his gaze on the door Jase used to leave the cafeteria.

CHAPTER FORTY-SEVEN

Jase sat at his desk, textbook open and sharp pencil ready. All he wanted to accomplish was to get this day behind him.

Students clamored in, Harrison in the mix.

Mrs. Ruppert, 2.0. How's that for a decimal?

She walked to the center of the room and looked down at a crumpled wad of paper in the floor. She snapped her fingers at the boy in the front row and pointed at the paper.

He jumped up and handed it to her.

She turned on her lime green flats and strode to the desk where she sat, straightened the collar of her orange turtleneck and began smoothing the wrinkles from the twisted mess.

The entire class sat in frozen fear as Mrs. Ruppert, without moving a muscle, raised her glare from the paper on her desktop to the frightened faces of third period algebra. Her eyes roamed the class, to and fro, examining each face.

"Who does this belong to?" She questioned.

Not a sound could be heard.

"I said. Who does this belong to?" She raised her voice ever so slightly.

"I'm going to send this piece of fine art around the room. I expect one of you here knows who the originator might be. I expect to hear from you by the end of class. Today's assignment is on the board. Get to work."

His eyes told his brain what the paper held, but his brain didn't want to believe it.

Someone had drawn a picture of Mrs. Ruppert. She wore a striped dress and tennis shoes. Her nails were like talons, her lips exaggerated in size, and her hair, piled in a high bun on the top of her head, was tied with a leopard print bow. Printed below the grotesque picture—Mrs. Ruppert, Queen of Mean and the Voice of Pain.

Wow. Some poor sap is in big trouble.

He passed the paper back and without another thought went back to work.

Mrs. Ruppert continued the stare down. Some wiggled and squirmed in their seats, others never looked up.

One stood and walked to the front of the room, right up to Mrs. Ruppert's desk.

Harrison Peterson.

A hush fell across the room as barely audible remarks could be heard.

"Oh, really?"

"Are you sure?"

"Thank you for your honesty."

"I will be sure Mr. Tims is fully informed."

Harrison cut his eyes at Jase and smiled as he strolled back to his desk.

The temperature in the room dropped fifty degrees the moment Jase's view moved from Harrisons wicked grin to Mrs. Ruppert's icy expression.

CHAPTER FORTY-EIGHT

"Are you sure Mrs. Ruppert was looking at you? You said you couldn't hear what the boy said, right?"

"I guess I can't be positive she looked at me. My gut tells me Harrison is up to no good."

"Well, your mom and Sully get home tonight. Try not to worry about what you don't know."

"I'll try, Pop."

Jase walked outside with Chesty. He tried not to worry but all the questions scrolled through his mind like the ticker at the bottom of the television screen when there's breaking news.

"Chesty, something isn't right. Harrison got here, and I tried to help him. I ended up in trouble. What changed while I was at the Table of Shame with Andrew? The only thing I can think of is Harrison. I don't know what he said or why, but one by one my friends are turning on me. Even Haley. And now this with Mrs. Ruppert. I know he told her I drew the picture. I'm innocent, Chesty. But how can I prove it?"

Chesty ran ahead and circled back, running around Jase and barking. Jase took a ball from his jacket pocket and tossed it. Chesty took off to get it.

I think Harrison wants to get rid of me. I think he wants my seat at the table.

Chesty dropped the ball at Jase's feet, wagging his tail so hard he almost knocked himself off balance.

Harrison is causing trouble between my friends and me. But why?

Chesty nudged the ball causing it to roll in front of Jase's foot.

"Hey, buddy! You brought it back! When did you figure out how to fetch? Good job!"

Jase tossed the ball once more. Chesty barked and ran full speed toward his target, tumbling over himself when he tried to slow down. He retrieved the ball and pranced back, with his head held high.

"Well, aren't you the proud one." Jase laughed.

Even as he laughed, he heard Mrs. Zimmers voice. *Hold your head high and keep your sense of humor. Everything will be okay.*

"What time will Mom and Sully get home?"

"Flight got in an hour ago. They should arrive any time now." Pop reached and patted Juju's hand.

"I hope they had a great time and will come home stress free. Somehow, when adults are stressed, I get in trouble."

"That pump knot on your head is still angry. Your momma might never allow us to look after you again."

Her comment brought the auto-response of reaching up to touch the goose egg.

"Aw, you don't need to worry. She knows how crazy my dreams can be."

"Hey! Hey, anyone home?"

"They're home!" Jase rushed to the family room.

The evening was filled with stories and laughter, and "I missed you and look what we brought you."

"How soon do you have to go back to work?"

"I have tomorrow off, but poor Sully has to return to the jungle." Janice talked about the trinkets she brought back for her coworkers and how much fun she'd had finding the perfect gift for each person.

"How's your week been? Everyone surviving okay?"

"We've had a wonderful time with Jase. He wasn't a minute's trouble." Juju's eyes twinkled.

"Sully, your parents came by for a visit Sunday afternoon. They said they wanted to get to know me before they had to leave. They didn't say where they were going."

"I'm glad they came by. I think you would like them if there's ever a chance to spend more time with them. How has school been this week? Keeping out of trouble?"

"School is school, what can I say? I have a group project due tomorrow in literature. I got to illustrate a scene from *The Book Thief*."

"How about lunchtime? Everything okay?"

"Especially lunchtime. Everything is fine."

Jase excused himself and stepped into the kitchen. He decided to clean up the supper dishes for Juju. Maybe Sully and his mom would go back to telling stories and laughing and forget about school until tomorrow.

He went to bed thanking God for his mom's safe return home. He prayed for his friends. He asked God to help him know what to do. He even prayed for Harrison.

And he prayed for Sully to be fair and patient while they were getting used to whatever this new life was going to be.

When he closed his eyes to sleep, all he could see was Mrs. Ruppert in a striped dress, wearing tennis shoes, with her hair piled high on her head. The Queen of Mean.

He rolled to his side and pulled Chesty in close.

"I didn't do it," he whispered.

CHAPTER FORTY-NINE

"Will you still be here when I get home from school?"

"I'm afraid not, we need to get back to the farm."

Jase hung his head.

"Now, now. Don't be sad. I'm sure you'll come to see us soon. Maybe we can arrange for you to stay with us during the summer." Juju squeezed Jase's arm.

"That's right. You can even bring your best friend. Sean? Stuart?"

"Maybe, Pop. Or maybe I'll come alone." Jase hugged Pop and hurried out the door to the bus stop.

The crisp January air must have caused the burning in his eyes. What else would explain the tears he wiped away before reaching the bus stop.

He didn't stay a word when he got there. Instead, he pulled his wool hat down and his collar up and shoved his hands into his pockets. He put his back to the group of used-to-be friends and watched for the bus.

Haley frowned at Steve. He threw his hands in the air with a what-do-you-want-me-to-do-about-it gesture.

Obviously, Danny and Deirdre were comfortable in their own world.

"Hey." She said, stepping in front of Jase. "Are you still speaking to me?"

"I never stopped."

"So ... how are you?"

"I'm fine."

Haley knew him well enough to know 'I'm fine' meant give me space.

She stood nearby until the bus arrived. All the while, she wished she had the right words to make this mess go away. She missed mornings full of laughter. She missed lunches full of conversation.

She needed to know everything was going to be okay.

Blazing red eyes.

Grunts.

No words.

Just grunts.

Jase followed Mr. Tims to the empty algebra classroom. Sully interrupted science class and asked to speak with him.

The picture. He must have heard about the picture. What else could it be?

Sully paced and grunted. Jase sat down.

But I didn't do it. He didn't even ask. I DIDN'T DO IT!

"Jase, I thought I made it clear to you last week. What's gotten into you? Are you trying to make me the laughingstock around here?"

"Sully, I ..."

"We are at school. How many times do I need to tell you? It's Mr. Tims."

"Mr. Tims, I didn't do it."

"Mrs. Ruppert explained the entire thing to me. She said Harrison Peterson saw you with the picture at lunch.

He saw you drop it on the floor. Why, Jase? Why did you do it?"

"I'm telling you the truth. I didn't do it."

"Go back to science. Principal Drew will be the one to decide how to handle this ... at school anyway. I'll deal with you later."

Jase stepped to the door and stopped. Without turning around, he said, "Mr. Tims. I did not draw the picture no matter what Harrison Peterson said. I don't know why you don't believe me."

And he returned to class.

"He says he didn't do it. But Janice, there's an eyewitness." Mr. Tims spoke on his cell phone and paced.

"I know this doesn't seem like Jase, but neither did the shoving match last week ..."

Up one aisle of desks, down another.

"Principal Drew will call him to the office later and handle school discipline. You and I need to decide what to do at home."

Mr. Tims stopped in his tracks.

"Well, I just thought ... I know I'm not his dad ... I'm telling you just like you asked me to ... Okay. Okay. Okay, then. We will talk later."

CHAPTER FIFTY

Miss Teal clapped her hands together and slightly bounced on the balls of her feet.

"This is going to be such a fun class project to share with one another. Who wants to go first? Come on now, don't be shy!"

No surprise to Jase, Madeline raised her hand and simultaneously sashayed to the front of the room. She snapped her fingers at Jase and Harrison, and they jumped to it like trained seals.

"We chose *The Book Thief*, by Markus Zusak. The story follows our protagonist, Liesel Meminger, during the terrible days of World War II. Liesel is fascinated by the power of words and is driven to read. There are several themes in this historical fiction, but the one I see the most is love. We can use our words to overcome even the most terrible experiences. We can use the power of our words to take care of each other and build strong friendships."

Madeline nodded at Harrison. He stepped up and announced the page number for the passage he chose to recite. Miss Teal followed along with her hand on her heart. With near perfection, he told of the day the Nazis marched the Jewish prisoners through town and the trouble that followed when a young boy tried to give a weak man a morsel of bread.

Jase displayed his drawing.

"This is Liesel as she gazes at the home of the Hubermann's, the people who fostered her during the horrors of the Nazi regime. She didn't know how to read and write when she arrived but learned while there. Liesel was surrounded by sorrow and death but gained hope through the power of words."

Miss Teal sniffled and patted the corner of her eye.

"If you choose to read this book, you will see the story is narrated by Death. I chose to give Liesel victory over death in my rewriting the end of this powerful story. You see, I believe if we use the power of words as Liesel chose to use them, we can find friendship and freedom and we never need suffer another World War."

She read her alternate ending, dedicated to the text even when her voice quivered. She pressed on and finished strong.

"Bravo! Oh, bravo!" Miss Teal clapped and cheered her approval. "Do the three of you recommend *The Book Thief* to your classmates?"

"Oh, yes! The story is beautiful and sad and powerful." Madeline shined.

"Um, yeah. Me, too. I think we can learn from historical fiction." Harrison mumbled.

"I had a hard time finishing it because I didn't want to learn the truth about what happened to people, especially the Jewish people, during the war. But when I finished. I was glad Madeline made us ... I mean we chose this book. I think everyone should read it." Relief washed over him. Relief to have the presentation over. Relief to no longer be in a group with Austin Justin Harry Harrison.

He returned to his desk. He would have enjoyed his relief if it weren't for one thing. Madeline's voice ringing in his ears, talking about the power of words to bring friendship and freedom. He glanced over his shoulder at Austin Justin ... Harrison. He looked at Harrison and couldn't help but wonder, are there any words that could possibly bring friendship with a guy bent on hurting other people?

CHAPTER FIFTY-ONE

When a guy has no appetite, he skips lunch and hangs out in the library. When a guy is hanging out in the library to avoid uncomfortable cafeteria moments with MIA friends, he doesn't expect to learn anything. But everyone knows, there is much to learn when in the library.

He perused the shelves, in search of a quick read. World War II nonfiction? Maybe historical fiction? Better yet, how about a graphic novel?

Too involved in reading title after title, he stumbled over some guy seated on the floor. A book slipped from the guy's clutches and slid across the aisle, stopping with a thud as it hit the shelf.

"Andrew? Are you okay? I didn't even see you."

"Yeah, yeah. I'm fine. You should maybe watch where you're going next time."

"I didn't expect anyone to be ... never mind. Why aren't you at lunch?"

"Why aren't *you* at lunch?"

"Not hungry, that's all."

Andrew glanced at the clock above the door. "I got to go. Watch where you're going, K?"

He left before Jase could answer. Getting back to his title search, Jase's toe bumped the book Andrew had been reading.

The Art of Friendship.

His stomach burned. His head pounded. Maybe he could call home and tell his mom he needed to rest his goose-egg head. Would that get him out of algebra? Doubtful.

Boom-boom, boom-boom. Each beat of his heart sent a percussion of pain from the front of his head to the back. *Chin up, Jase. Head held high. Go with the flow and roll with the punches.*

Determination flowed through his veins. Determined to prove his innocence. Determined to prove he was a man of integrity. Determined to make his stepdad/teacher learn the truth.

Determination is more determineder when a guy is in the hall. There must be an invisible vacuum that sucks determination completely out of the same guy when he crosses the threshold into class. Not just any class. The class led by the stepdad who disbelieves. The class with the accuser seated in the back row.

So much for determination.

"Let's not waste any time this afternoon. You'll complete a chapter review worksheet during class and turn it in before leaving today. If you do not finish, you will have algebra homework. Be warned, though, I will deduct five points on all worksheets turned in tomorrow."

He didn't smile. He showed no emotion. And he wasn't amused when Mandy asked a question.

"Mr. Tims, aren't you going to ask what went wrong while you were gone?"

"Not today, Mandy. I've been informed about all that went wrong while I was away." He cast his gaze from

Mandy to Jase and lingered for a moment. "Get to work. I'd prefer not to deduct points on students because they failed to focus."

Whispers upon whispers, classmates hissed their complaints.

"Way to go, Jase."

"What a loser."

"I hope the drawing was worth it."

"That will be enough talking. Would you prefer I just go ahead and deduct five points today?"

Like a mallet striking a podium, his heart reminded him with each beat in the center of his blue forehead—Sully had assigned himself judge, jury, and executioner.

And now he could add his algebra classmates to the list of people angry with him.

CHAPTER FIFTY-TWO

If someone had told him over Christmas break he would end up seated across from Principal Drew before the end of January ... well, he wouldn't have believed it. And if he had been told he would warm this chair twice in January? Naw ... not in a million years.

"Principal Drew, what can I say to prove I did not draw the picture of Mrs. Ruppert?"

"We have a witness."

"Yes, sir. I've been told. And I don't know why he would lie. I give you my word. I did not do it."

Principal Drew rapped his knuckles on his desk and sighed before spinning his chair around to pause as he looked out the window behind his desk.

"Weren't you here just a couple of weeks ago? Seems I remember you and Andrew and the Table of Shame. Bet you didn't know I know that's what you kids call it. The Table of Shame."

Jase barely moved. Hardly breathed. His statue-like outer appearance cloaked the scrambling going on in his brain.

"Now that I think of it," Principal Drew continued. "You were in trouble for helping Harrison Peterson."

"Yes, sir. And now Harrison Peterson is the witness. But he isn't telling the truth. I didn't do it."

"I don't see why he would lie about this, especially after you helped him. I imagine it pained him to tell on you."

He didn't speak again. He sat and he waited.

What will the punishment be today?

In-school suspension?

More Table of Shame?

Maybe something new, like cleaning all the whiteboards for his remaining days at CMS.

"Go back to class, Mr. Freeman. Come see me tomorrow at lunch time, and I'll let you know how this will be handled."

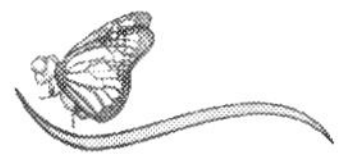

He slung his backpack onto his bed and kicked his shoes off. There were no words to describe the anxiety building in his chest.

Every bounce of his seat on the bus ride home reminded him he was one bounce closer to being dealt with by Sully and his mom. The aroma of supper in the crockpot turned his stomach as he imagined a very uncomfortable meal around the table.

"Jase, come set the table."

For a moment he considered pretending he didn't hear her. After all, she's in the kitchen and his door was closed.

Instead, he moped his way to whatever the future held.

Breathe in.

Breathe out.

"Want to talk about it?"

"Talk about what?" *Does she know? Did Sully tell her?*

Breathe in.

Breathe out.

"Sully called today. He told me what happened."

"Mom, I didn't do it."

"Sully thinks you ..."

"Harrison is out to ... what?"

"Sully told me you deny drawing the picture. He thinks you're guilty."

"He told me he believes Harrison. He wouldn't even talk about it or hear me out."

"I know, Son. Let's give Sully another chance, okay? He's had time to think. Tell me about Harrison."

"He's new. Came after Christmas break. Haley invited him to sit with us at lunch. All I know is, everything has been falling apart ever since."

"Everything is a big word."

"Okay, well ... maybe ... no. Everything is the right word. School, friends, and now home. That's pretty much everything."

"We are going to work *everything* out together. As a family. Sully ..."

"Is angry. Very angry. He thinks I am trying to cause trouble for him."

She reached out and pulled Jase close, giving him a tight squeeze. "Look at me, Son."

He didn't want to look. He didn't want to see whatever was in her eyes. He didn't want to disappoint her. He never meant to cause trouble for Sully, but he would *never* make life difficult for his mom. Not on purpose anyway.

They couldn't finish their conversation. The click of the lock on the front door sounded.

Sully was home.

CHAPTER FIFTY-THREE

She met him at the door and leaned in.

"Let's wait and talk with Jase after supper, okay?" she whispered. Turning away from him, she raised her volume, "Supper will be ready in fifteen minutes."

The only sounds that could be heard once Sully blessed the meal were forks scraping plates and plunks of glasses touching down on the table. The occasional 'please pass the salt' broke the silence.

She watched her son taking his time to eat and wished she could hear his thoughts.

Across the table sat Sully. She wondered how this icy wall between him and Jase could have formed so quickly. She spoke to God in her heart and asked him to melt the wall and bring peace to her new family.

Sully didn't know what to think or say. This kind of stress so soon after the wedding was the last thing he wanted.

He thought he knew Jase. Jase's behavior and what he knew just didn't add up. He'd spent all afternoon replaying recent events. Jase and Andrew in the hall, the shoving match. Harrison telling him what Jase did wasn't necessary. And now this. A disrespectful picture of the sub while he was out of town. Jase is a good artist. The picture was a sloppy sketch, not quite Jase's style. But the witness ... Harrison. *Why is Harrison around when trouble is present?*

Jase took another bite of spaghetti and twirled the next bite around his fork. He chewed slowly, hoping to make his plate of food last until bedtime. Maybe, just maybe, Sully and his mom would decide to let it ride. Or maybe some good news would make the inevitable conversation less painful.

"We earned an A on our group project in literature. Remember? *The Book Thief*. What a great book. It's one of those stories you can't stop thinking about once you've read it."

"I always enjoyed historical fiction, especially Civil War era stories. I imagine World War historical fiction would be no different. Those books have a way of making the reader experience history." Sully sounded like the old Sully. Not the angry Sully.

"I don't think I knew about this project. Tell me about it." Mom leaned forward and placed her elbows on the table.

"Miss Teal put us in groups of three. We had to choose a book to read and then each of us had to make a presentation."

"Sounds like a fun project."

"Pretty much. If ya like group stuff."

"Who was in your group? What did you do for your presentation?" Sully sipped his tea.

And at that moment, Jase wondered why he chose to make conversation by telling them about the project. He dropped his head and closed his eyes.

"Well, uh, my group leader was Madeline. Not because we asked her to be, she kind of just took the lead." Jase examined his spaghetti, turning his fork again. "And Harrison Peterson."

"Harrison has a way of showing up around you." Sully's voice remained calm.

"I … uh, illustrated a scene from the book." Spin, spaghetti, spin.

"I hope I get to see the picture. You are an amazing artist." *So much pride in her voice.*

"I'd like to see some more of your work as well." Sully didn't look at him.

Janice cleared her throat and cast a frown in Sully's direction.

Spin, spin, spinning spaghetti.

"Is your illustration a pencil sketch or watercolors? Tell me more."

Jase readjusted himself in the chair and tugged at his collar.

"I chose pencil sketch because the mood of the scene, and really the entire book, is serious. I'm sure Miss Teal will return the picture later. May I be excused?"

He didn't wait for an answer. He took his plate to the sink, scraped it, and loaded it into the dishwasher. He thought about going to his room to wait for the hammer to fall. Instead, he turned to Sully.

"I think we need to talk."

"I suppose we do."

"Sully, you're going to believe whatever you choose to believe." His voice was steady. Respectful. "Do what you gotta do." Jase didn't look away. Instead, he stood tall. Shoulders back. Head held high. And he looked Sully square in the eye.

"Your mom and I will talk and let you know."

CHAPTER FIFTY-FOUR

Muffled voices.

Whispers.

Louder. Then softer.

Silence.

His door creaked open, and they stepped in.

He waited.

He had already decided he would not say a word. Whether the truth ever came out or not, he knew the truth. And today, that's all that mattered to him.

"We've decided you will be grounded until Monday. That means you will miss the first basketball game of the season. Before you get angry, you need to know your behavior this entire school year makes the accusation believable. I'm sorry, Son." She kissed the top of his head and walked out.

He bit the corner of the inside of his lip and counted the small holes in the toe of his left sock.

Sully stepped forward and held out his hand. Jase relinquished his cellphone.

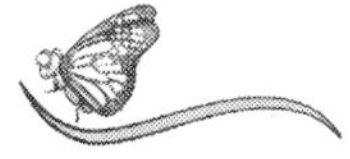

Muffled voices again.

This time he could understand them.

"Maybe, just maybe, we should have started our first week together as a family by standing with Jase. Can we be one-hundred-percent sure he is guilty?"

"You know we can't. But think logically for a moment. He's been in trouble several times this year. Harrison, who has no reason to lie, said he saw Jase draw and drop the picture."

"Forgive me, Sully, but you have chosen to believe a new boy you hardly know over the word of Jase. Jase hasn't lied to either one of us. He's been honest about everything that has happened this school year. Not to mention all the changes in the boy's life. I don't think you have put much thought into Jase's perspective."

"Janice, I ..."

"Sully, I'm not asking you to believe Jase isn't capable of making big mistakes. I'm asking you to give him a chance before you condemn him."

The tree outside his window swayed with the winter wind and bowed under the weight of the snow resting on its limbs.

His warm breath fogged the cold windowpane. He strained to see a star, just one star. But the night sky was shrouded by winter clouds.

A starless night. Seemed fitting. Even so, he refused to let all the stuff he didn't understand erase what he learned from his dad through the many letters he had tucked safely in a box in his closet.

When you don't know what to do, do what you know to do.

He remembered having to reread the sentence several times before it began to make sense.

He did not know what to do about Harrison, the picture, his friends, or Sully.

So, he did what he knew to do.

Get ready for bed.

Read his Bible.

Say his prayers.

Trust God to work it all out.

Get up tomorrow and go to school with his head held high and believe everything would be okay. He decided to tone down his sense of humor for a while.

And, of course, he would go with the flow and roll with the punches.

CHAPTER FIFTY-FIVE

"Yes, sir. I'll get right on it." Principal Drew handed her a piece of paper containing a list of names.

She stepped to a microphone, mashed a button, and spoke with a cheery singsong voice, "Excuse me, Miss Teal? Is Haley Brown present?"

"Yes, ma'am, she is."

"Please send her to the office."

She shivered.

Her hands were iced.

Her toes tingled.

The blood drained from her face and pooled in her belly, causing a wave of nervous nausea. She had never heard her name followed by a request to go to the principal's office.

Her frigid fingers interlaced, she stiffly walked the long hall to Principal Drew.

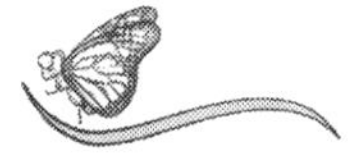

He stood near his favorite window, warming his hands with his coffee cup. He inhaled the rich aroma of the strong black liquid. He turned when he heard her at his door.

“Come in, Haley. Have a seat.”

She robotically obeyed.

“How are you this morning?”

“I ... uh ... I’m ... I was okay. Until a few minutes ago.” Her fingers hurt, yet she twisted them a bit further.

“Oh, no, no, no. Don’t be nervous. You are not in trouble.” He chuckled. “I just need to ask you a few questions, okay?”

“Okay. Yes, sir.” She twisted her hands one more time.

“Whatever you say to me stays in this room. I know you are good friends with Jase Freeman. He’s been accused of something, and I am investigating. Has he told you about what happened?”

“Um ... no, sir.” Uneasy tears spilled out and tiny rivers traced her cheeks.

Principal Drew handed her a tissue and said, “Why does my question upset you?”

“Well, Jase and I haven’t spoken much recently. Ever since ...”

“Ever since?”

She looked up at Principal Drew and whispered, “Harrison Peterson came to CMS.”

“Oh? Why would Harrison’s presence change how often you and your friend speak?” He raised both bushy eyebrows.

“That’s a good question, sir. I don’t know the answer. All I know is, I invited him to eat with us, and we’ve had nothing but trouble since.” She wiped away the tears with her arctic, achy hands.

“You’ve been very helpful. Are you okay to return to class or do you need a few minutes?”

She stood and inched her way to the door. “I’m okay.”

“Be sure you get a permission slip to return to class. Mrs. Thomas will help you.”

"Dr. Drew? I hope Jase isn't in trouble. I don't understand or know what's going on, but I know Jase. He's not a bad person."

"Thank you, Haley. Don't you worry."

She nodded and stepped out of his office.

Once in the safety of the hall, Haley leaned against the wall and willed her hands to stop shaking. She searched for reasons Jase might be in trouble. She couldn't explain what happened to him or her friends, but she knew something was terribly wrong.

She began the walk back to class and hoped her stomach would stop flip-flopping.

And then she heard it.

Mrs. Thomas's smiling voice chirped over the speaker in the hall, "Steve Snyder, please come to the office. Steve Snyder. To the office."

He sipped his now lukewarm coffee and grimaced.

He imagined little Jase Freeman entering kindergarten just a few years ago. He remembered how pleased the teacher was when Steve Snyder befriended the frightened boy. Kindergarten certainly was a difficult year for a boy without his dad.

A wave of pride washed over him as he thought of how far Jase had come since then, from fear to fearless. From timid to bold in entering his slogan in the Bully Free Zone contest. Not just entering but winning.

Jase was a smart, successful, and yet typical middle school boy. Yes, perhaps in a moment of lost self-control he created the drawing. But Principal Drew had a feeling the puzzle pieces didn't fit.

Haley Brown confirmed there was more to this story than one witness and an accusation.

CHAPTER FIFTY-SIX

"What ya got there?" Coach K towered above Mr. Tims's desk.

Mr. Tims, hunched over papers, rubbed his chin. "It doesn't make sense."

Coach leaned in and examined the papers for himself.

"If you're about to tell me you're going to give up teaching algebra for art class ..."

"You're ridiculous. Look at these. What do you see?" Mr. Tims slid the papers so they laid side by side.

"Hmm. I see an illustration created by someone with a lot of talent. And I see a haphazard, sloppy, scrawled mess that could have been found in any trash can at Crumberry Elementary School."

"Exactly. Makes no sense. I asked Miss Teal for Jase's assignment he turned in yesterday." He pointed to the art. "Jase has been accused of this act of disrespect." He handed the caricature to Coach K.

"Nope. I don't see it. These two were not created by the same hand."

"Unless he was in a hurry. Or is clever enough to draw a big mess on purpose so he wouldn't be a suspect."

"You don't really think Jase ..."

"I don't know what to think."

"I've known Jase a long time, Sully. He's a typical kid, not perfect by a longshot. But I don't think he would do this."

Sully held the two drawings up to the light and shook his head.

"Coach, I've made a big mistake."

"Welcome to parenthood, bro." Coach palmed Mr. Tims on the back.

"Any advice?"

"Sometimes you gotta eat some crow to get the respect back." Coach K stepped into the hall. "Tell the kid you're sorry. Make it right."

Sully took in a big breath, held it, and gradually blew the air out.

He would worry about crow pie later.

If Jase didn't draw the picture, who did?

CHAPTER FIFTY-SEVEN

"Good morning, Mr. Snyder. Take a seat."

Steve sauntered in and sat on the edge of the chair, looking around Dr. Drew's office.

"I like what you've done with the place, Dr. Drew. You have style." Steve's toothy grin brought a large smirky return from Principal Drew.

"I'm glad you approve. How are you feeling? Any more headaches?"

The reminder of his football concussion acted like a giant eraser sweeping over his face, removing any sign of a smile. "I'm fine. No more headaches. Is that why I'm in your office?"

"I'm glad to know you are well. I need to ask you a few questions."

"Well, why didn't you say so. How may I be of service to you?" Grin. Returned.

"Jase Freeman."

Grin. Removed.

"Why the frown? I thought you were best friends."

"Well, can I be totally honest with you?"

"I expect nothing less."

"Jase has changed. He's acting like he's the stuff, ya know? Like maybe Mr. Tims marrying his mom makes him special or something." Steve shrugged. "And don't forget what he is going around saying. I don't know if he thinks shooting his mouth off makes him look good to the new kid or what."

"Oh? What has he said to you?"

"He hasn't said anything to me. He said stuff about me."

"Did you somehow hear him say this stuff?"

"No. But a trustworthy source told me what he said."

"More trustworthy than your best friend?"

"Former best friend. Out with the old, in with Harrison ... I mean, the new."

"Just like that?"

Steve fidgeted in the chair. He curled his lip and glanced at the strange pictures on the wall. "Interesting paintings you have there." He nodded toward the art.

"Thank you for your help, Steve. You may return to class."

"Oh. Okay. That's it? That's all you need?" Grin. Again.

"Yes, we are finished."

Steve stood and extended his right hand. Principal Drew smiled back at him and shook hands with the goofy young man.

He watched Steve leave and chuckled as he overheard, "Hey there, Mrs. Thomas. You sure run a tight ship around here. Good job."

He reached for his cup and went in search of a fresh pot of coffee.

Mr. Tims: Do you have a few minutes? I'd like to speak with you before you meet with Jase

Principal Drew: Yes, if you can come now

Mr. Tims: BRT

Principal Drew: Huh?

Mr. Tims: Be Right There

Principal Drew: Oh

"I'm not convinced Jase is guilty."

"We're on the same page. I'm doing a bit of investigating, myself. What do you have?"

Mr. Tims placed the two pictures on Dr. Drew's desk. "Look at these. What do you see?"

"Hmm. I see what you mean. Where did you get the pencil sketch? It's quite good."

"Miss Teal let me borrow it. Jase sketched it for a group project in her class. They earned an A by the way." Mr. Tims puffed up with pride.

"I can't imagine this artwork earning anything less. This though." He held the crude drawing of Mrs. Ruppert. "While the other is a sketch, this is clearly a scratch. I think I know where you are going with this."

"Right?" Mr. Tims examined the two pictures again, as if he were looking at them for the first time.

"Did you say the art is part of a group project? Who was the rest of the group?"

"Let me think. Jase said her name is Madeline Jones. And Harrison. Harrison Peterson."

"Really, now. Our only witness to Jase's crime? Interesting." Dr. Drew stood back and placed his hand on his chin in an I'm-thinking-kind-of-way.

"I've got to get back to class. Houston is doing crowd control for me. I'll check back with you later." Mr. Tims stepped away but swiftly turned back. "Dr. Drew. I can't afford to make big mistakes so soon with my new family. If Jase did this, he needs to learn the seriousness of disrespect. But if he is innocent ..."

"I agree. Check back with me later. I'm supposed to meet with Jase during his lunch hour."

Mr. Tims left the dueling masterpieces on Dr. Drew's desk and scurried away.

He sat at his desk and glanced over the new evidence. He scratched his head and leaned back in his chair. Working with middle school kids challenged and tested him. Even so, he placed importance on being fair and making a point of knowing the facts before handing down a ruling.

"Mrs. Thomas, please call Madeline Jones to my office."

CHAPTER FIFTY-EIGHT

He tried to focus.

He really did.

But how can a guy focus on science when his fate hung in the balance? Science somehow didn't matter today.

Science.

Forensics.

Fingerprints.

Proof.

Get a grip, Jase. Just do the next right thing. Focus.

"I'm Madeline Jones. You called me to the office?"

"Hello, Madeline Jones. Principal Drew would like to speak with you." Mrs. Thomas gestured toward Dr. Drew's open door.

She knocked three times before stepping in. "Excuse me, Principal Drew? You wanted to see me?"

"Yes, yes. Hello, Madeline. How are you this morning? I hear you just completed a group project in literature. Can you tell me more?"

"Yes, we earned an A! We read *The Book Thief*. Jase Freeman illustrated a scene, I rewrote the ending, and Harrison Peterson memorized a passage."

"Ah, yes. I know both boys."

"Jase was great. He listened and went along with what I suggested. Harrison, well, Harrison almost messed us up."

"Oh?"

"He acted like he didn't care. Honestly, I didn't know how serious I was going to have to be. I told him not to bring my GPA down with his foolishness."

"Are Jase and Harrison friends?"

Madeline half shrugged. "I don't know. They didn't talk to each other much. Our project was all business, Meet, decide, work. Wait ... Jase got sassy with Harrison in our last meeting. I didn't know why though. He treated him with contempt."

Principal Drew cloaked his surprise with her vocabulary. He imagined Madeline would one day own a Fortune 500 company. He would read about her in the financial section, and she would employ thousands.

She shifted her weight, one foot to the other. She crossed her arms and noticed Dr. Drew's choice for office decorations.

"Van Gogh or Gauguin?"

"Picasso."

"I should have known. Picasso had his own way of interpretation." She nodded toward his desk. "Thinking of adding to your collection? Jase is a future rock star in the world of art."

Principal Drew stacked the papers and slid them into a folder.

"You're right. He does show promise. Thank you, Madeline. You may return to class."

"I'm not sure what I did, but you're welcome."

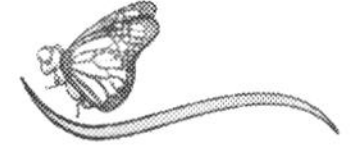

Jase settled into his seat in literature. Easy hour ahead. He could relax and listen to the remaining presentations.

No worries.

Until lunchtime.

"Hey, Jase. Congrats."

"You too. I doubt we would have earned an A if you hadn't been so boss ... I mean if you hadn't taken charge."

"Yeah, a body with no head is useless, but a body with three is freakish. So, you're welcome. But I'm not referring to our grade. Principal Drew has your illustration from our project. You've impressed him."

"Huh? Oh, uh ... yeah. Right."

That's just weird. Why ... what does it matter?

The tic, tic, tic from the clock above the door ticked a bit louder with each passing second. His blue goose egg pulsed with each tic.

Soon enough, he would know his fate.

CHAPTER FIFTY-NINE

He wondered if anyone knew.

Was anyone at Crumberry Middle School aware of all the trouble in his life? Well, anyone other than Austin Justin Harry Harrison. Harrison knew.

This is ...

All.

His.

Fault.

Each step toward the office made his blood boil at a higher temp. After all, he wouldn't even be taking this stroll if it weren't for Harrison's meddling. Who does he think he is, anyway? Coming in here, messing with his friends? Screwing up his life?

He tasted blood and realized he had chewed the inside of his lip. Funny how a guy can allow anger to get the best of him.

Easy, Jase. Self-control. Go with the flow.

"Hello, Jase."

Jase sat and waited. Intent on keeping quiet. Self-control meant no smart mouthing the principal, especially in his office.

"I've done some looking into what happened Tuesday. I have an idea, but I need to ask you not to tell anyone."

Curiosity cooled his steaming temper down to a simmer.

"You will spend your lunch hours tomorrow and Friday in my office."

"Sir?"

"Don't ask questions. Just come to my office. And tell no one. In fact, start today. I'll ask Mrs. Thomas to bring you some lunch. Yes. Yes, I like this idea. Just sit tight."

"Principal Drew, I don't understand. If you think I'm innocent, why am I being punished?"

"You aren't being punished. Think of it as ... well, more like protection. If you're in my office, you aren't around whoever set the trap for you to be blamed. Just a few days. You can do this."

And just like that, he left his office.

Jase twiddled his thumbs and tapped his foot. He checked out the ceiling and counted the tiles.

He stood and stretched. What time is it? How much longer must he endure the orange shag carpet and super-odd prints that represent the best of the world of art?

Get real, Jase. What's worse? Old orange carpet or algebra? The stare down from weird art or from classmates?

"Brought you some lunch," said Mrs. Thomas. "Be sure you eat. No matter what is going on, take care of yourself. Eat." She sat the tray on a table near a bookshelf.

Is this what it feels like to be held against your will? Stranded in a sea of orange shag carpet with a tray of cafeteria food quickly growing cold.

Given a choice though, this is way better than algebra. Principal Drew had not even asked him if he'd rather miss algebra or lunch. What's up with that?

They sat at their usual table in their usual spots.

Danny and Deirdre, focused on their food.

Haley rested her chin in her hands, wishing she had an appetite.

Steve, moving his lunch around on his tray like it is part of an edible Rubik's Cube.

Jase's empty seat screamed his absence.

"Hey," Steve whispered. "I got called to Drew's office this morning."

"Seriously?" Haley answered, hushed and a tad excited. "Why? Are you in trouble?"

"Naw, he just asked me a few questions."

"I wonder what's going on around here. I got called too."

Harrison arrived, slid his tray over, and sat in Jase's empty seat. "Who called you? Anything exciting?"

Haley chose not to answer. She was too busy over thinking every conversation with or about Jase from the past week. Especially her trip to the principal's office.

Harrison sat in Jase's seat, munching away at his lunch like everything in life is grand, but Haley wished she could rewind to the day she met him.

If she had a do over, she would never invite Harrison Peterson to lunch again.

Steve had his own moment going on, which he knew was a rare thing. He preferred to joke around and keep it light. You know, don't worry, be happy and stuff like that.

Today was different.

Principal Drew had questions. Haley had questions. Now, he felt some questions popping up in his own brain.

He peered at Harrison Peterson, sitting in Jase's seat. He couldn't help but begin to think Harrison might have answers.

CHAPTER SIXTY

Sometimes a guy needs to take his time getting to class. Especially when that class is algebra. Especially when the class is taught by the guy's new stepdad. And especially specially multiplied ten times when the guy's stepdad/teacher is an angry stepdad/teacher.

Jase sat and exhaled a sigh without a sound.

Get in. Do the work. Keep quiet. Get out. Could there be a better plan?

If someone had asked him if he could possibly get through an algebra class without a word, he would have said no way.

And if someone had said the brightest spot in his day would be getting through an entire algebra class without a word ... well, who needs a day when the brightest spot isn't bright at all?

So close.

He kept his nose clean and to the grindstone, eyes on work. Mouth shut. And moments before the bell, he looked up to see the face of angry stepdad/teacher hovering above his desk.

"Sir?"

"I have meetings after school. I probably won't get home until after supper, but we will talk then, okay?"

"Okay." Back to the grindstone.

A guy can look like he's concentrating on his work when in reality he's asking himself a hundred and one questions about why his angry stepdad/teacher didn't seem so angry anymore.

Has he already decided to extend my grounding into eternity?

Maybe he is going to give me the "I'm so disappointed in you" speech.

He could be putting together a plan to make me clean school bathrooms or scrape lunch trays until the end of the school year.

He imagined himself scraping disgusting left over sloppy joes and peas or maybe that gross green jiggly stuff into trash cans of epic grossness even pigs wouldn't eat.

He wondered if any CMS student ever broke enough rules to deserve such cruel and unusual punishment.

And he wondered what his angry stepdad/teacher had in store for him.

"Can I go to church tonight?"

"Of course. You know you don't need to ask."

"Well, I'm grounded and all."

"Never from church. We'll leave in thirty minutes. Sully has meetings and won't be able to go with us."

Jase welcomed the chance to go to youth group. He always liked being there, but tonight was good for more than one reason. Every minute at church meant one less minute for possible conversations he didn't want to have. Seriously. How many times did he need to say "I'm innocent" before someone believed him?

He had invited Steve to come to youth group many times. Steve's answer was always the same, "Naw. Maybe another time."

He wondered if *another time* would ever arrive now that they were hardly friends.

The guys sat on futons in the center of the room. A few had open Bibles in hand. The small group leader led in prayer. Jase listened while Scripture was read, Matthew 6. He had heard the passage before. Had read it many times himself. But tonight, the words jumped off the page and seemed to scream at him.

Seek first the kingdom of God and his righteousness, and all these things shall be added unto you.

"How? How do you seek the kingdom of God? What's his righteousness? I'm confused."

What followed was a lively discussion of what it looks like when a middle school boy seeks God first.

"Bottom line, we seek God by reading the Bible and praying. We seek God when we decide to care most about what God wants and not what we want. When we put God first by using what we learn in Scripture to make a difference in our lives, we are seeking his righteousness. The words sound complicated when, in reality, the message is simple. This passage means to put God first, and he will take care of everything else."

Jase didn't think this passage sounded simple at all. He wondered how seeking God's righteousness would have made a difference in his current mess.

And he wondered if starting right now would make the truth known.

CHAPTER SIXTY-ONE

Like a get-out-of-jail-free card in Monopoly, Sully's truck was nowhere to be seen when Jase and his mom returned home from church. His long day left him very little self-control, but he managed to keep from shouting "YES!" After all, how would he explain that happiness to his mom?

Instead, he thanked her for taking him to church and said goodnight. He talked with Lecty and told her all about church and wanting what God wants. He also told her he wanted Harrison Peterson to ride off in the sunset, to disappear as quickly as he appeared.

The question weighing on his mind as he tried to fall asleep before the sound of Sully's truck pulling in met his ears was *can I seek God's kingdom and avoid Sully for as long as possible, or does avoiding Sully mean I don't care about what God wants?*

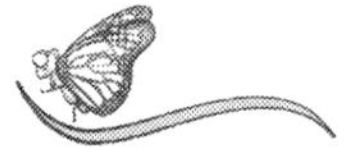

The last person to get on the bus that morning, Jase swelled with a bit of pride. Pride over managing to get out of the house without seeing Sully, and pride at timing his arrival to the stop just seconds before the bus pulled away from the curb.

No uncomfortable conversations.

No explanations.

He imagined today as a covert operation. Fly in under the radar, get the job done, and get out undetected. The job, and he had no choice but to accept it, was to remain alert and wait for the truth to surface. Oh, and yeah … keep his nose clean while rolling with the punches.

Did he know his imagination was going wonky on him? Yes. Did he care? No.

He did it on purpose.

The CMS hall rule has always been to stay to your right. Principal Drew explained the rule often during his morning drone of announcements.

"A steady flow of traffic gets us all to class on time. Stay to the right. Get there on time."

He obviously did it on purpose.

Veered to the left when he saw Harrison walking toward him. Well, okay. Harrison wasn't necessarily walking toward *him*, he was doing what he did every day at 10:05. Andrew knew Harrison's schedule. Walking the hallway at 10:05 meant literature class.

Today, it also meant a brief encounter.

Andrew's comparatively large shoulder collided with Harrison's. That's what happens when you move to the left when you should stay to your right.

Instead of walking on, Andrew's shoulder shoved Harrison to the wall, his literature book slipped from his sweaty palm and fell to the floor.

"Um, hey. Wh, wh, what's up?" Harrison's eyes darted back and forth.

"Harrison, I'm on to you. Just want you to know …" And he lifted his hand, pointed to his own eyes and turned his hand toward Harrison, pointing two fingers his direction.

"I don't know what you're talking about."

"Whatever." He repeated the gesture and walked away.

Harrison, visibly rattled, watched Andrew walk away. He gathered his book and continued to class with his right shoulder pressed against the hall wall until he arrived at the classroom.

CHAPTER SIXTY-TWO

Jase slid his carrots into his applesauce. He nibbled a chicken tender.

"Chicken tender. Why is it called a chicken tender? This one came from a tough old bird. Should be called breaded chicken jerky."

He spoke, but no one was there to answer. He sat alone in Principal Drew's office.

Mrs. Thomas scurried around the outer office stacking papers, answering the phone, and sending students here to there. She hummed all the while she worked.

He listened to her hum and wondered what makes a person happy enough to hum while working.

Time in this office inched along at the pace of a sloth in a race for his life. He dared not snoop or touch anything, but ... well, he was tempted to open a drawer or peek inside a folder. Teachers liked to mention the infamous "permanent record." Does a permanent record really exist?

The pesky little voice in the back of his head whispered and told him to look. The voice he had a choice of listening to or not urged him to do the right thing.

If he had not just been to church the night before and heard what it means to seek God first, well, he would have looked for his permanent record. Seeking God first won out, and he sat down.

The clocked ticked.

He reconsidered the applesauce-coated carrots and breaded chicken jerky.

"I'm not sure what you want me to do." Steve gulped his milk.

"I want you to think for a minute. Has Jase ever even joked about your grades or how smart you are? No. I don't think he called you a dumb jock."

"If he didn't, then why ..."

"I don't know yet. But we should pay attention. We need to fix this."

"What's broken?" Harrison arrived, grinning. "I'm pretty good at fixing things."

"I bet." Steve sneered.

"What's that about?" Harrison sat, in the spot he claimed in Jase's absence.

"Don't worry about him. He's hangry. Give him a minute to eat." Haley's eyes widened when she looked at Steve, giving him her best "play along" stare.

"Oh! Yeah. Yeah, that's all. I'm hangry." Steve chomped a chicken tender.

Harrison shrugged. "Okay, so what are you trying to fix?"

"Who broke what?" Danny and Deirdre joined the table of friends.

"I've been thinking," Haley raised her eyebrows at Deirdre as she spoke. "Jase. Jase has caused a lot of trouble lately. How can we fix him?"

"What? Jase hasn't ..." Danny's sentence cut short the moment Deirdre's foot contacted his shin under the table. "Ow!"

Harrison kept chewing. His face showed he was engaged in their conversation, but he didn't add to it.

"Harrison, are you listening? Jase needs fixing." Steve stood, casting the bait.

"Steve. Eat." Haley reached and pulled Steve back to his seat.

The two watched Harrison take a bite of chicken and reach to open his milk.

Haley placed her hand on top of Harrison's. "What do you think, Harrison? Do we need to fix Jase?"

He shrugged once more and kept eating.

Haley couldn't understand why Harrison didn't jump in and blame Jase for some dreamed up atrocity. A minute earlier, she thought he was at the heart of the messed-up friendships.

But there he sat.

In Jase's seat.

Eating without a care.

Eating as if all was right in the world.

No one but Harrison saw him.

Andrew.

Two tables away.

Listening.

Glaring.

Waiting.

CHAPTER SIXTY-THREE

"Hey, I looked for you this morning, but you were already gone to catch the bus. Let's be sure we talk this afternoon, okay?" Mr. Tims greeted Jase.

"Okay." Jase tried to smile.

Harrison walked by and said hello. Even asked where he was during lunch. Jase chose not to answer.

How can the guy lie about me and cause trouble for me and then look right at me and say hello? I don't get it.

"Pop quiz! Put your textbooks away and take out your pencils."

A couple of weeks ago, a pop quiz announcement brought protests. Today, the students knew better than to complain. Everyone knew Mr. Tims had quit playing around. And everyone blamed Jase. Better to suffer in silence than be on the receiving end of a grouchy teacher.

All eyes in the room burned right through his T-shirt, searing him like a branding iron. He wanted to turn and shout at them. He wanted to tell them to mind their own business.

How bad could it be? I'm already in trouble.

His mind took a quick trip to Release-land. The only place a guy could say what's on his mind without finding himself on lockdown. The imaginary words poured out and flooded the room.

Why don't you know-it-alls stick to algebra and keep your crummy noses out of my bubble? You don't even know who deserves your anger. Take a look at the new kid. He could decide to cause trouble for you next. Maybe you should dog-pile on Harrison. That's it! Ready, set, go!

Sometimes, he wished he could enjoy a hateful thought without the guilt. He heard his conscience loud and clear, reminding him his thoughts should seek God's righteousness and his actions would follow.

Sometimes he didn't appreciate knowing the right thing to do.

Instead of lingering in Release-land, he waited for the quiz paper. He decided to force his thoughts to seek God's righteousness. He also refused to give Sully another reason to condemn him.

And as hard as he tried to keep his cool, blotchy boy made another appearance. No doubt his accusers witnessed his scarlet ears and ruby neck. Did Harrison take extra pleasure in seeing him squirm under the weight of all the googly-eyes? He amused himself by remembering his Lapis Lazuli-blue goose egg. At least he had some blue splashed in among all the red tones.

What can a guy do when he doesn't know what to do except do what he knows to do? First, ace this quiz. Then finish the day strong and be ready for "the talk."

"May I use the phone to call home? I don't feel so great." Harrison placed his hands on his stomach as he spoke to Mrs. Thomas.

"Of course, sweetheart. Do you have a pass from your teacher?" She reached and touched his forehead with the back of her hand. "You don't feel feverish."

"Maybe it's something I ate." He handed her the hall pass.

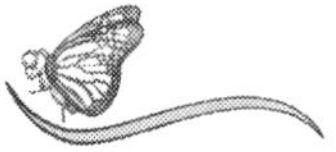

The basketball careened toward him. He jumped and tried to catch it, but it flew over his head, barely skimming the tips of his outstretched fingers. He chased after it, watching it bounce and roll out of the gym. The timing could not have been more perfect. Mr. Tims had just walked through the main entrance of the school, heading toward the parking lot. The ball sprang after him, following him out of the school like a puppy following her master.

Jase jogged after the ball and reached to scoop it up.

"I thought I told you not to call me at work unless you're bleeding. Are you bleeding? I don't see any blood." Her sharp voice carried through the air. "You better have a good reason for interrupting work. You're going to get me fired." She uttered a curse under her breath.

"I'm sorry but I ..."

"You're sorry? No. You're not sorry. Are you telling me you couldn't make it until the end of the last class of the day?"

"Mom, my stomach ..."

"Hardly an emergency. Just get in the car." She cursed again and slammed the car door.

He obeyed.

Jase held the basketball and his breath.

Mr. Tims stopped in his tracks. He and Jase locked eyes.

Tires screeching, the car sped away.

Jase carried the ball back to the gym. He couldn't get the sight and sound of what he witnessed out of his mind.

And no matter how hard he tried not to, he couldn't help but feel sorry for Harrison.

CHAPTER SIXTY-FOUR

"I'm no longer sure of your guilt and neither is Dr. Drew."

Jase sat up straight as Sully's words lifted his spirits.

"We aren't ready to reverse your grounding yet, but I want you to know Dr. Drew and I are investigating what happened."

"I know I haven't made the best choices this school year, but I'm telling you the truth. I didn't do it."

"The truth will be known. Be patient and let us find out who created the picture. We don't know very much about Harrison. It's hard to imagine why he would cause you trouble and scheme against you."

"I don't understand him either."

"We have decided you can go to the basketball game tomorrow night." Mom stepped into the room.

"Can I ask you a question? Why, after everything he has done to me, do I feel bad for Harrison?"

"Sully told me what the two of you heard this afternoon. I think you feel bad for him because you realize you don't know all there is to know about his life."

"I guess. I'm confused, though. Because I'm still mad at him and wish he had never come to Crumberry."

"Pray for him. God wants us to pray for those who hurt us." Sully sighed.

Jase rolled his eyes. He knew Sully was right. Even so, he didn't want to pray for Harrison.

Would it be okay to pray for the Peterson family to move away?

Jase: Hey

"Who is it?" Haley pushed in to try to read for herself.

"Just Jase. I guess he's trying again." Steve shrugged.

"What do you mean, again? He's been texting you? Have you answered him?"

"Yes. And no. I haven't had anything to say to him."

Jase: I get to go to the game tomorrow night. Maybe I'll c u there?

"What's he saying?"

"Not much. Says he's going to the basketball game tomorrow night."

"Answer him."

"Huh?"

"You heard me. Answer him."

"You're not the boss of ..."

"I'll do it." She grabbed his phone and began to text.

"Hey!"

"Don't worry. I'll let you read it before I send it."

Steve: This is Haley. We're glad you'll be at the game.

"Uh, are *we* glad?"

"Steve, it's time for you to grow up. Either send the text or write your own. But text him back."

Delete. Delete. Delete.

Steve: Cool

Haley looked on as he typed. She smirked and shook her head.

"What? I texted."

The after-school activity bus pulled to a stop on Juniper Street.

"Steve, we've got to fix this. You have to admit; Jase has always been a trustworthy friend."

"Truth."

"And he's always had your back."

"Truth again."

"He isn't perfect, but ..."

"You can say that again."

Haley puckered her lips and raised one eyebrow.

"Sorry. Truth. Is that better?"

"Much. Now go home and figure out how we are going to fix this." She didn't even slow her pace as she turned and walked to her front door.

"Yeah. Okay. Whatever." Steve mumbled.

"I heard that!"

Steve didn't look back. He began the short jog to the end of Juniper Street and his warm home waiting for his return from a long school day.

He lingered at Jase's house. He kinda sorta wished he could go knock on the door and invite himself to supper, just like old times.

Instead, he replayed every conversation he'd had with Harrison from the first day back from Christmas break until today. He replayed conversations he had with Jase as well, or at least he tried.

For the first time since their friendships began to crumble, Steve realized he had hardly spoken to Jase at all.

CHAPTER SIXTY-FIVE

"Hey, Pop. What are you doing?"

"Oh, we just finished supper. I'm glad you called. Have you had a good week?"

"Well, if you define good as I'm still breathing, I guess it's been good."

"That rough, huh?"

"Yeah. I've been in trouble all week, and I didn't even do anything wrong. That kid, Harrison, planted a picture he drew of a teacher, and I got blamed for it. I'm grounded. My friends think I'm a jerk."

"You're right. That's a rough week."

"I figured you could tell me what to do."

"You're not going to like what I have to say."

"Say it anyway."

"Sometimes you just have to be quiet and patient and wait for the truth to surface."

"What about Harrison? I hate that kid."

"Hate is a mighty strong word."

"I know. I'm sorry, but I'm just being honest."

"Do you see Harrison much during the school day?"

"He's in two of my classes."

"Maybe you should try being extra nice to him."

"Huh? I don't feel like being nice to him."

"Sometimes you need to act your way into feeling and stop waiting to feel your way into acting."

"You're more confusing than seeking the righteousness of God."

"I have some homework for you before you go to bed."

"Seriously? That's not why I called."

"You called for answers. Instead of getting answers from me, you can get them from God. Read Psalm thirty-four. You're going to see that being righteous means you choose to do the right thing. You don't have to be Harrison's best friend, but you do need to be kind to him. Read chapter thirty-four. And tomorrow, do the right thing. What do you have to lose?"

"So go with the flow, roll with the punches and do the right thing?"

Pop laughed as he spoke, "Read Psalm thirty-four and ask God to help you. Psalm thirty-five is pretty good stuff, too."

"We better get off the phone before you ask me to read the entire book."

"Good night, Jase. Juju and I will be praying for you. Turn to God first and everything will be okay."

"Good night, Pop. Thank you."

"What's wrong with Jase?" Juju twisted her hands and stood next to Pop as he sat at the table.

"He's learning hard life lessons. But you and I know God is using every difficult experience to make him more like Jesus. Jase will see God is always working."

Juju patted Pop's hand. "I'm so glad we have you, Pop." She kissed the top of his head. "Now how about you help me clean up these dishes?"

"Old woman, you sure can get bossy."

She smiled. "Old man, don't you forget it."

CHAPTER SIXTY-SIX

Lapis Lazuli.

The universal symbol of wisdom and truth.

If rocks could speak, what would this perfectly gold-speckled, bluest-blue stone say? Don and Margo said the Lapis Lazuli is just a rock with no special powers. He remembered what they said about paying attention to the Creator of the stone.

Jase rolled the gem across his knuckles and back. No powers and yet, the symbol of wisdom and truth. He needed a truckload of both.

Maybe if he tucked the smooth rock under his pillow, he would wake up tomorrow knowing how to catch Austin Justin Harry Harrison in his own trap. How cool would it be to have an easy fix from a magical stone?

He rubbed the stone between his thumb and fingers.

Sully said to pray for Harrison.

Pop said to read Psalm thirty-four and be kind to Harrison.

They both said the truth would somehow be known.

God? I don't exactly know how to pray for Harrison. I saw what happened with his mom today. My mom has never cussed at me. Poor guy just had a stomachache.

But Lord? He's not just a poor guy. He's a troublemaker. So, I guess I'll pray for you to arrange for the truth to be known. And please help me to keep my mouth shut. I'm really good at making a bad problem worse. Help me do the right thing. Amen.

He shoved the stone under his pillow. Why not? Is there anything to lose?

He flipped open the Bible Juju gave him and searched for Psalm thirty-four. He tried to focus on verse one, but his eyes were drawn to verses thirteen and fourteen. A bright yellow highlighter made the passage impossible to avoid. Had Juju underlined the verses? Or maybe his dad marked the words because he wanted to remember them. Either way, Jase was certain Pop knew the verses were marked.

Keep your tongue from evil. Turn away from evil. Do what is good. Seek peace. Pursue peace.

He patted the bed and Chesty obeyed. "Kinda hard to look for peace right now. Everywhere I turn, evil seems to be staring me in the face."

Chesty sneezed and plopped down next to him.

As badly as he wanted to close the Bible and just go to bed, he forced himself to read chapter thirty-four.

The eyes of the Lord are on the righteous ...

The Lord is near the brokenhearted ...

The Lord redeems the life of his servants, and all who take refuge in him will not be punished.

He retrieved the bluest blue nugget from under his pillow and placed it back in the box. He believed what he read. Leaving the Lapis under his pillow meant his refuge was in a rock. He chose not to trust in a rock, but to trust in God.

The loud voice at his locker might as well have been a fist to his face. He walked up in time to see Steve emptying all of his belongings from their shared locker.

"What are you doing? Why?" Jase's mouth went dry, and he choked on his own words.

“Don’t talk to me. I thought you were my friend.” Steve’s voice dripped with scorn and grew louder with each syllable. Middle school kids stopped and stared.

“What are you talking about?”

“I said don’t talk to me.” He shoved the final book in his backpack.

“But ...”

Steve stepped nearer to Jase and looked down at him. His eye’s reminded Jase of the eyes of a hawk in a picture he saw once of the hawk swooping down on a rabbit.

“Steve?”

He whispered, “Harrison told me this morning. He told me everything you’ve said. I thought you were my friend.” And he walked away.

You would expect a guy to be upset about what happened. Maybe wish he could find a place to cry. But Jase didn’t feel like crying. No.

Punching back.

He needed to punch back.

CHAPTER SIXTY-SEVEN

He pushed through the crowded hall, searching for one cowardly face. All he needed was a split second and he didn't care what Dr. Drew or Sully could do to him.

He tried to stuff the silent voice in his head telling him his plan to hit back wouldn't end well. He fought against his conscience, urging him to stop. A fleeting plea flew through his head, asking God for help to do what is right.

He barreled around a corner and slammed into the chest of Andrew.

"You need to get outta my way."

"No, I don't think so."

"What did you say?"

"Let me help you, Jase. I've been watching. I've been listening. I know what he's doing to you."

Jase stepped back and slowed his breathing. A stream of angry sweat ran from his hair across his goose egg, burning. He wiped the wet away before it reached his eyes.

"Just give me today. Let me help."

Jase bit the inside of his lip and dug his fingertips into his palms.

"Do what you need to do to stay away from Harrison."

Jase tried to speak but no words worth saying came to mind. So, he clenched his teeth, nodded at Andrew, and walked away.

Mr. Houston's furrowed brow stopped Jase at the door. "Son? Are you okay?"

"I'm fine." Jase tried to walk to his desk.

"Hold it right there. You're not fine at all."

"I will be. Just had a bad start to my day. That's all."

"Take your seat. Breathe. I don't know what happened this morning, but whatever it is, it will pass."

Jase wondered if Mr. Houston would say the same thing if he knew all there was to know.

He sat.

And he breathed.

And as he began to calm down, he remembered what he read the night before.

Turn away from evil and do good.

"Excuse me, I need to get to my locker." Harrison spoke to the back of a student much larger than himself.

Andrew turned around.

"Oh. Hey, Andrew." His voice, less than confident.

"I told you I'm on to you. I know more than you think. I'm going to be sure everyone knows."

Harrison pursed his lips and shrugged. "I'm not worried about you or anything you have to say. Why would anyone believe you? Did you forget already? You're the one who bullied me my first day here. The entire school knows it."

"I'm smarter than you think. I know you planted that picture and blamed Jase. I know you're lying to his friends. Everyone will know soon exactly what kind of person you are."

"How would you know what I have or haven't done? Did you see me or hear me?"

"No, I didn't see you with the picture. But I know you did it." Andrew stepped closer to Harrison.

"Yeah, I did it." Harrison whispered. "But you'll never prove it."

"Jase tried to be your friend. They all did. I don't know why you are doing this to them. But they need to know."

"Go ahead. Try to tell them. No one cares what you have to say. No one will believe you. You're a nobody."

Harrison left his locker without getting any books.

Andrew reached into his pocket, pulled his cellphone out.

He smiled as he stopped recording.

Jase didn't believe Andrew stood a chance at helping. But he was thankful. Thankful Andrew bought him time to calm down. Time to remember who he is and whose he is.

Jase knew Andrew stopped him from making a very big mistake.

CHAPTER SIXTY-EIGHT

One more hour.

Just one more hour in wall-to-wall shag carpet.

He had no appetite.

Jase sat, staring past Dr. Drew at work behind his desk, to the window behind him. The view made the world seem calm. New snow had fallen through the night. The blanket was undisturbed. Jase didn't even see a bird in flight.

Peace.

Stillness.

So unlike the start of this school day.

He managed to keep from looking at the face of Harrison during literature class. Much to his surprise, Harrison didn't speak his empty greeting. In fact, Harrison didn't even pass by his desk. Jase saw from the corner of his eyes, Harrison took the long way to be seated.

Odd.

Yes, definitely odd. But one more reason to be thankful.

"Jase?" Dr. Drew interrupted his trance. "I've come to the conclusion you did not draw the picture of Mrs. Ruppert. I have no evidence to prove who did, but you did not. You're free to go to lunch."

"Are you going to tell Sully ... I mean Mr. Tims?"

"We've already spoken. He agrees with me. He said he will speak with you later."

"Thank you, Dr. Drew."

Jase spoke to Mrs. Thomas as he exited the office. She wished him a great day.

He was glad for the first step in vindication, but his feet remained heavy.

The weight of all those who didn't or don't believe him pounded down inside his sneakers. He imagined leaving giant indentations in the floor as he didn't even try to step lightly.

So, he is no longer in trouble for something he shouldn't have been in trouble for in the first place.

How would his release from orange carpet mend his friendships?

How could a future conversation repair what he used to have with Sully?

And what can be done about Austin Justin Harry Harrison?

"Hey, you guys, first game tonight! I'm nervous about keeping the books. Ya know, I've never been on a team before." His tray in hand, he scanned the remaining empty seats around the familiar table and sat next to Danny.

"You'll do fine." Haley didn't look up.

"Technically, I'm not sure keeping books makes you a part of the team." Steve's cold voice chilled the cafeteria air.

"Ouch," Harrison's eyes narrowed.

Clinks of forks on trays and grunts, sighs, and stares followed.

"I haven't decided yet. Might not go to the game." Steve's frigid words broke the conversation silence.

"I never planned to go in the first place. Colossal waste of time." Deirdre whispered.

"Please change your mind. I want to go, but I don't want to sit alone." Haley pleaded.

"You're asking a lot of our friendship." Deirdre frowned.

"At least you still have a friendship." Steve blurted.

And more silence followed.

Haley pushed her lunch tray to the center of the table. She wondered how this happened to her friends, whatever *this* is. She looked her friends over.

Steve, rambunctious, always joking and forever hungry Steve, sat with his chin resting in his hand. He wasn't even looking at his food.

Deirdre, logical and happy Deirdre, didn't look up from her food.

Danny, agreeable and kind Danny, took precise bites of tater tots.

Jase's empty seat.

Harrison, the one she hardly knew, munched his food and bobbed his head like he could hear music no one else could hear. Not a care in the world Harrison.

Wait. What? Jase's empty seat?

But why is he no longer sitting in Jase's empty seat?

Jase spent the rest of the lunch hour walking in the gym. He had no energy to run. No one spoke to him. Not even Coach K.

Thankful for a few minutes of solitude, he repeated what he knew to be true. One word for each step he took.

Turn. Away. From. Evil. And. Do. What. Is. Good.

CHAPTER SIXTY-NINE

Relief washed over him when he walked in the front door and realized he made it through the day without punching Harry in the face.

In fact, the rage he experienced this morning was no longer surging through his veins. He wondered if this is the meaning of Psalm 34. His quick call for help. Did God send Andrew his way?

Starving from a skipped lunch, he found his way to the kitchen for a sandwich.

He heard the front door and assumed his mom had come home from work.

"I'm making a snack. Want some?" He called out.

"Sure," Sully stepped in. "I could use something to eat. I missed lunch."

Jase wasn't sure he wanted to snack with Sully right now. Sully. The one who believed the worst of him. Sully. The one who wouldn't listen. Sully. The punisher.

"I'm here to say I'm sorry."

Jase studied the makings of his sandwich and continued piecing the snack together. Had he heard correctly?

"I should have listened to you. I should have relied on what I know about you and given you the chance to explain. I'm sorry."

He swallowed hard. He definitely heard correctly.

"You know, Jase, sometimes adults make mistakes. I'm not afraid to admit when I'm wrong. Can you forgive me?"

"I know I haven't made the best decisions lately. I'm sorry too." Jase sat down and slid a sandwich to Sully.

"We need to move forward and do what we can to make our new family strong."

"Yeah. Yes, sir. I'll do my part."

"Do you forgive me for doubting you?"

"Yes."

Jase felt the air get lighter with each bite he took. He wondered if Sully felt it too.

"Sully? I'm glad the picture stuff is cleared up. But my friendship with the gang is still a mess. I don't know what to do. I don't know how to stop Harrison. I tried to be his friend."

"I know you did. Some people are mean. I think you need to accept the fact that you can't change Harrison. You can't do a thing about the way he treats you. You can only control how you respond."

"You sound like Pop. Haley tried to be his friend too. Why is he causing problems for everyone who has tried to be his friend?"

"Maybe he's never had a real friend. Maybe he doesn't know how to be a friend."

"I'm sure he knows he is causing trouble. I wanted nothing more than to hurt him this morning."

"I'm glad you didn't."

"Andrew stopped me."

"Andrew?"

"Yeah. He asked me to trust him."

A few bites later, Jase asked if he could still go to the game, and Sully agreed to take him. Maybe he would have a chance to thank Andrew after the game.

"Go ahead. Try to tell them. No one cares what you have to say. No one will believe you. You're a nobody."

Haley and Steve stood motionless as Andrew played the conversation for them.

"I don't know what to say." Haley spoke stoically.

"Well, I do. Where is the little pipsqueak? I can take care of this right now. Who does the punk think he is?" Steve began to pace.

"No time. The game will start soon. We can take care of him later." Andrew dropped his cellphone into his gym bag.

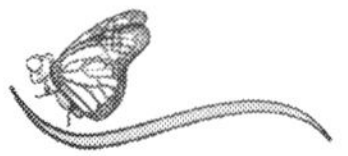

Harrison took his place on the bench. He sat tall with pride at being a part of the team. He didn't care what Steve said. He was wearing a jersey and is sitting near the water bottles marked with the CMS Wildcat's logo. He certainly was part of this team.

CHAPTER SEVENTY

"I'm not sure where I'll sit tonight. Maybe I should forget the game and stay home."

"That's an option, but why should you stay home? There's a whole school full of young people to choose from. Probably a few kids who are just like you. Wishing for someone to hang out with."

"Maybe."

Sully pulled to the front of the school. "Text me when you're ready to come home. I'll see you later."

"Thanks."

Jase stood at the door to the school and took a deep breath. He exhaled and summoned the courage to walk in, friends or no friends.

He reached for his ticket money and his cellphone vibrated.

> **DON:** Jase, this is Don Tims. Sullivan gave me your cell number. Margo and I just finished praying for you. I want to remind you to trust in the Lord alone. He is Truth. No need to text me back. Margo and I are soon to depart for a remote area, and we must leave our cellphones behind. Pray for us as we pray for you—that God would cover you in his mercy and protection. Until we meet again, know you are precious to our Father.

That was nice. Kinda odd. But nice. I wonder where "remote" is ...

He purchased his ticket and made his way into the crowded gym. The game had already begun, and the Wildcats were in the lead.

He searched for a place to sit. Not alone but not anywhere near the gang. He spied Madeline and her friends. She was turned so she could talk to the girl on the other side of her, Madeline's back was to him. He sat down anyway.

The crowd screamed when Andrew's three-point shot swooshed through the net. Madeline stood to cheer and spilled her nachos on Jase's head.

"Oh! Oh, no! How long have you ... I'm sor ... Oh, no." She covered her mouth, mortified eyes peering above her hands.

"I just got here." Jase picked a nacho from his hair. "This is gross. Want me to bring you more nachos after I get cleaned up?"

"That's nice of you, but no. I should be offering to get you something."

"Do you care if I sit here for the rest of the game? Steve and Haley aren't talking to me much."

Her perplexed expression caused him to regret asking.

"Jase, you know how people talk. Everyone has heard the rumors. *All* of them."

"Yeah, well I didn't do anything wrong. So just forget it."

Jase made his way to the restrooms, hearing comments such as "cheese head" and "mousetrap" as he passed by. Cheese-sauced hair and anger are not a good mix.

I wonder if glue is really white nacho cheese sauce? Maybe I should have flung some of this at the jerks in the gym.

Chip by cemented chip, he peeled the food from his hair. Rinsing in the sink proved to be little help. The yellowy-orange color was gone but the yuck remained. So, he made the best of a sticky situation, and using his fingers like a comb, spiked his hair into a Mohawk.

Not bad. A new me?

CHAPTER SEVENTY-ONE

He tossed a piece of popcorn high into the air, tilted his head back, and caught it with ease. Chomping on the hot, buttery, saltiness almost distracted him from what waited in the gym.

With each kernel he tossed into his mouth, he listed one more unbelievable change since Christmas break.

Crunch. Mom is married to my algebra teacher.

Munch. Steve is mad at me.

Chomp. Two trips to the principal's office.

Nibble. Sully believed the accusations Harrison Peterson has made.

Grind. Sully believed the accusations Mrs. Ruppert has made.

He stopped eating when a thought seeped into his mind and turned the buttered popcorn to greased rocks sitting in the pit of his stomach.

Mom. Mom hasn't had his back even one time. Has anyone had his back? No.

He crumpled what was left of the popcorn bag and tossed it into the trash. Standing just inside the gym, he watched students laughing and goofing off, only half watching the game. He wondered if he would ever goof off and half watch a game ever again.

Principal Drew conversed in a corner with a few parents. Principal Drew might be the only one who believed him.

Now at least. At first, he was all "you've made some bad decisions lately, Mr. Freeman."

He spied Harrison, seated at the bench. Looking all official. Happy and proud. Like he belonged at CMS.

The soles of Jase's feet burned. Heat sailed up the back of his legs and scorched the back of his neck. Scarlet freckles grew in size until they meshed together to form the mottled return of blotchy boy.

The heat traveled until his eyes burned.

Tap.

Tap, tap.

"Jase."

Tap.

"Hey. Jase?"

She shook his shoulders. "Jase!"

"What?" he scowled when he turned around, super annoyed to have his vengeful stare disrupted.

"Walk with me." Haley ordered.

He followed.

Steve stepped from around the corner.

"Okay. What? Are you going to gang up on me? Who is going to hit me first? I'm sure I must have done something terrible again. I mean ..."

"Be quiet." Steve spoke in a weird, hushed tone.

"What?"

"Jase. I'm sorry. We were wrong. So wrong." She twisted her foot back and forth.

"What?"

"She's right. I'm sorry, too. I should have known better. I should have talked to you, asked you."

"Yeah. You should have."

"What more can I say?"

"Why do you all of a sudden believe me? What changed?"

"We don't have time to explain all that right now. I don't know how we can fix our friendship. But tonight, we are going to fix Harrison." Steve hissed.

"What?"

"After the game. Andrew and me, we're going to give Harrison a taste of his own medicine."

"Wait a minute. You never said ..." Haley put her hand on Steve's arm.

"Don't go getting soft. Think about all the trouble he caused. He deserves whatever Andrew and ..."

"What does Andrew have to do with this? And I agree with Haley. You can't ..."

"I don't need your approval. Neither does Andrew. Harrison made a fool of us. You can meet us at the lockers after the game or you can go home. I don't care either way. I just wanted to say I'm sorry." He pulled his arm away from Haley and walked toward the gym.

"I don't even know what to say right now."

"Jase, please forgive me. I'm sorry."

"I forgive you. I don't have the energy to hold a grudge right now. Not against you anyway."

"Are you, um, are you going to go?"

"Go where?"

"The lockers." Haley shoved her hands into her pockets and looked at her feet.

"I dunno. Maybe. Harrison is a jerk, might be good to see him get what's coming to him."

CHAPTER SEVENTY-TWO

One by one, the lights in the halls dimmed.

He felt the grip on his collar and knew he was helpless against it. Pushing his heels onto the slick tiles in hopes of slowing the pace proved unsuccessful.

Andrew slung Harrison against the lockers and held him by his shoulders. Steve cast a shadow ten feet long.

"Hey! Get your hands off me!"

"You don't get to tell me what to do." Andrew sneered.

"Hey there, buddy. Andrew played a recording for us. I'm thinkin' I heard your greatest hits or somethin'."

Harrison's eyes shifted, and he licked his lips. "Yeah, well I don't know what you're talking about."

"Yeah, I did it. Go ahead. Try to tell them. No one cares what you have to say. No one will believe you. You're a nobody."

Harrison swallowed hard.

"You're a real piece of work. What I don't get is why? Why did you cause so much trouble for us?"

"I think you need a pounding." Andrew pulled back his fist.

"Wait! What are you doing?" Jase rushed around the corner.

"Like we said, Harry here needs to learn a lesson." Andrew did not remove his gaze from Harrison.

Jase tried to step between them. "You can't do this. It's wrong."

"Wrong? Don't you remember what happened the last time you defended this guy? The Table of Shame. Seriously when all our troubles began." Steve raised his voice.

Harrison's mouth went dry, and his eyes darted. "Maybe, if you give me a chance, I can explain."

"Naw, we don't care what you have to say. We know what you've done. Jase, you probably ought to get out of the way so you aren't hit by a stray fist. Andrew is pretty mad."

"I'm not moving." Jase stood firm.

Andrew lowered his fist. "Have you forgotten everything this guy did to you? He lied. A lot. He planted that picture for Mrs. Ruppert to find. He even made your dad ..."

"Step. He's my stepdad."

"Sorry. Your stepdad. He lied to him too."

"Jase, think about what he did to all of us. Haley tried to be his friend, and all he did was mess with her. He messed with me." Steve's voice quivered.

"Andrew, I know you're looking out for me, and I'm glad. But you can't do this. It isn't your place to even the score. Steve, don't you get it? Hitting him won't fix anything. It will only get worse."

"I thought this is what you wanted," Andrew let go of Harrison. "You need someone to stand up for you. You don't deserve what this punk is doing."

"And you don't need more time in Principal Drew's office."

Steve stepped closer, "You're one lucky troublemaker. You better know, I don't think like Jase. I think you deserve exactly what Andrew said. A pounding."

Harrison tugged on his team T-shirt, smoothed it out, and looked from face to face to face.

"Let's get outta here." Steve set his sights for the parking lot.

Andrew inched closer to Harrison and whispered before following Steve. "I'm not finished with you."

Jase turned to Harrison, "I hope you know how bad that could have been for you."

"What do you want? A thank you? You're not getting one. I didn't ask for your help, so forget it."

"I don't want anything from you."

"Well, what are you looking at?" Harrison's eye twitched.

"If ever a guy deserved a poke in the eye with a sharp stick, it'd be you."

"Good one, Jase. Next time try to be original."

"Leave me alone, Harry. Find a new group of friends."

Harrison stepped away but stopped and looked back. "You really think you're special, don't you? Crumberry. This town is for losers."

CHAPTER SEVENTY-THREE

He sat at his desk, the cedar box containing his dad's letters from war opened on his lap.

He had already read each one several times. The words his dad penned gave him courage through many difficult moments when Steve was in the hospital a few months ago. These envelopes also held laughter and tears. Jase knew he could turn to the advice and stories his dad recorded in the event he did not return from Afghanistan.

Here he sat.

Rereading them yet again.

His confusion over the events of not just what happened after the game but since school resumed after Christmas break overshadowed him like a heavy curtain. He had questions. So many questions.

Why?

Why had Harrison chosen him?

Why?

Why did Harrison cause trouble between him and his friends?

Why?

Why did Harrison lie?

The words on the frayed paper he held in his hands were as fresh to him as if they were today's newspaper. Most letters were buried deeply into his memory, word for word, because he purposed to remember his father's words and instructions.

And yet.

What is this? Nestled in the middle of recollecting a lesson learned the last summer his dad played little league ball, his questions were answered. Sort of.

> ... the guy was just plain mean, Jase. I never knew from game to game if Nick was my friend or no better than an opponent. I asked your Pop about him, told Pop there was no rhyme or reason to his hatefulness. I'll never forget what Pop said. "Some folks are mean, and that's all there is to it. Why? Only God knows. Your job is to do the right thing."
>
> Pop reminded me before each game to be a team player and remember who I am and whose I am. Honestly, sometimes that was the only reason I didn't punch Nick right in the throat.

Wow. A punch in the throat? Harsh. Some folks are mean. And that's all there is to it?

He took great care to fold the letter and place it in the envelope. He tucked the envelope into the cedar box.

Even as grateful as he was for the words from his dad, he longed to hear his voice. If only he could talk with his dad one more time. How he wished he could tell him about the changes that had taken place and even all the ways God had taken care of them since ... since the news of his death.

He is a proud son and would be sure his dad knew of the pride that welled inside his chest.

Determination.

Determination to do the right thing even when he wanted nothing more than to seek revenge.

He remembered who he is and whose he is, and he knew deep down in his heart, acting on the truth—this is what made him a man.

He slid the small cedar chest across the top of his desk and right into the box holding his Lapis Lazuli stone.

The small box fell to the floor, the lid glided one direction as the box skidded another. The stone rolled with surprising speed until it rested under his bed.

Jase carried the cedar box of letters to his closet before scrunching down to retrieve the runaway Lazuli. The tips of his fingers barely touched the gem, but he stretched and rolled the bluest blue into the palm of his hand.

CHAPTER SEVENTY-FOUR

He examined the blueness, marveling again at how one small stone could be bluer than any blue he'd ever imagined.

Even more mind boggling, God created this blue beauty on purpose. A stunning example of his creative powers.

He could hear the voice of the man with the whirly twirly mustache, "*If you read up on gems, you'll learn Lapis is a universal symbol for wisdom and truth. We couldn't think of a more perfect gift for you as your family begins a new chapter.*"

The woman with the hair, forever curled and motionless, had also spoken. Her gentle but confident voice resonated in his head. "*This stone is described as timeless blue. When you look at it, we want you to be reminded God is truly timeless. He never changes. In fact, an important part of his message to us is he will always be who he has always been. You can count on God.*"

Jase placed the bright blue jewel in its resting place.

He knew.

God, truly timeless and unchanging, had shown him truth and wisdom. Perhaps Harrison Peterson was just plain mean. Or maybe there was more to his story than anyone at Crumberry Middle School knew. Either way, Jase would go to school Monday morning and give Harrison the "hey, what's up" nod, smile, and go his way.

He would thank Andrew for looking out for him.

He would find Principal Drew, acknowledge all he did to uncover the truth, and express gratitude for being more than the voice of morning announcements and keeper of hallway traffic.

And he would take his seat at his table of friends, knowing no one is perfect,and he could forgive the misunderstandings between them.

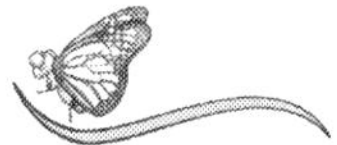

Margo placed her hand in the crook of Don's elbow. They stepped off the plane and took in the view of the land that lay before them.

The expanse of bright blue as far as the eyes could see offered hope of life to the desolate hills below. Hills and more hills, still covered in rock and dotted sparsely with rebellious green sprigs rolled beyond the horizon.

"Mr. Tims, are you ready for a new adventure?"

"Why, yes, Mrs. Tims. With you and the good Lord, I am ready for whatever awaits."

He had not yet discovered that something had tumbled from the lapis box, nestled in between the wall and the leg of his desk.

Parchment, fragile with age, and precisely folded. Scrawled on the silent lineless surface, a cryptic message meant only for the holder of the timeless blue lapis lazuli.

EPILOGUE

The mother duck waddled to her place of rest under the Dogwood tree in full bloom. Her brood of ducklings moved in double-time to keep up. As soon as she sat and puffed up her feathers, they gathered around her, snuggled under her wings, and shielded themselves from the chill of the spring breeze.

"I'm pretty sure this is the coolest treehouse ever."

"Right? I told Pop you would want to move in." Jase eyed Pop and Juju's house as he looked out the window of the best treehouse in the universe. After the events of the past, he thought Steve would never be around to enjoy this view.

Steve ran his hand along the smooth windowpane. "Hey, listen. I ... well, like I've said a million times, I'm really sorry. I don't know why I believed Harrison."

"All is forgiven. Let's put the mess behind us. Seems he's moved on to other prey now."

"I kinda feel sorry for the guy. I mean, why. Just why?"

"I don't think we'll ever know the answer. I do know one thing, though. I'm not going to let him make me act like him. I could easily be mean to him. But I'm going to go with the flow, roll with the punches, and do the right thing."

"You're a funny little guy, you know that? Wait, no. I'm not gonna call you a little guy ever again. You're one of the biggest people I know. I think your dad would be proud of you. I don't think I would have been man enough to stop Harrison from the beating he deserved."

Jase watched the mother duck with her little ones. He thought of how she protected and cared for them. He spoke a silent prayer, thanking God for protecting and caring for him by giving him Pop and Juju. And, of course, his mom, who's always in his corner.

And he thanked God for Team Tims.

Movement in the tree above the duck family caused Jase to look toward the dogwood blooms. And there it was. Perched on a bloom at the top of the tree, oh so gracefully and slowly fanning one wing. A beautiful, multi-colored, bulgy-eyed butterfly. Jase stood at attention, smiled, and saluted back.

ABOUT THE AUTHOR

Shelley Pierce lives in the Smoky Mountains of East Tennessee, where she enjoys her work as Preschool & Children's Ministry Director at Towering Oaks in Greeneville. She and her husband, Tommy, enjoy being grandparents to seven and counting. Author of the award-winning middle-grade fiction series, *The Crumberry Chronicles*, as well as picture books *I Know What Grandma Does While I'm Napping* and *High-Water Hattie*, she retreats to write at every opportunity. She released her first middle-grade nonfiction title, *Get Off the Struggle Bus*, in February, 2021. Shelley is also the author of Sweet Moments: Insight and Encouragement for the Pastor's Wife. Connect with her at https://pierceshelley9.wixsite.com/mysite and www.inthequiver.com

OTHER BOOKS—SHELLEY PIERCE

CHILDREN'S BOOKS

I KNOW WHAT GRANDMA DOES WHILE I'M NAPPING

HIGH-WATER HATTIE

Middle Grade Books

The Crumberry Chronicles

NonFiction

Get Off the Struggle Bus

Adult

Sweet Moments: Insight and Encouragement for The Pastor's Wife